DID ✹ YOU ✹ KNOW ✹ . . .

✹ Sometimes a mile wide and several times taller than the Empire State Building, the funnel of a tornado can wipe out an entire town in seconds.

✹ Some scientists purposely put themselves in the path of a tornado in order to learn more about it.

✹ History's first "tornado chaser" was Benjamin Franklin, who pursued a small whirlwind on his horse, snapping his whip at the storm.

✹ Scientists have speculated about "killing" tornadoes by dropping monstrous balloons into the funnels.

✹ A tornado's violent winds can toss railway cars around like toys and shoot straws into trees and playing cards into metal.

✹ The tornadoes in the movie *Twister* never really existed—except inside a computer.

Learn all this and much more in this fascinating book of amazing facts.

TWISTER

THE SCIENCE OF TORNADOES AND THE MAKING OF AN ADVENTURE MOVIE

Abridged Edition

KEAY DAVIDSON

A MINSTREL® BOOK

Published by POCKET BOOKS
New York   London   Toronto   Sydney   Tokyo   Singapore

WORLDWIDE PUBLISHING™

*This book is dedicated to the memory
of Dr. Arnold Shankman,
a historian, teacher, and friend
who departed this life much too soon.*

A Minstrel Book published by
POCKET BOOKS, a division of Simon & Schuster Inc.
1230 Avenue of the Americas, New York, NY 10020

TWISTER copyright © 1996 by Warner Bros. and Universal City Studios, Inc.
Copyright © 1996 by Keay Davidson
Photos from the motion picture by David James and Ron Batzdorff copyright © 1996 by Warner Bros. and Universal City Studios, Inc.
Back cover photo copyright © 1989 by Roy L. Britt/Weatherstock

This is an abridged version of the Pocket Books trade paperback edition.

All rights reserved, including the right to reproduce this book or portions thereof in any form whatsoever. For information address Pocket Books, 1230 Avenue of the Americas, New York, NY 10020

ISBN: 0-671-00396-8

First Minstrel Books printing September 1996

10 9 8 7 6 5 4 3 2 1

A MINSTREL BOOK and colophon are registered trademarks of Simon & Schuster Inc.

Text design by Stanley S. Drate/Folio Graphics Co., Inc.

Printed in the U.S.A.

ACKNOWLEDGMENTS

First, thanks to my family, particularly my sister Georgia "Tina" Davidson, a fellow tornado buff. She gave me the idea for this book. Second, to Phyllis Heller, who encouraged me to stick by the idea when it was lost at sea, and who steered it toward the right agent, Jane Cushman. And third, to my boss Phil Bronstein at the *San Francisco Examiner*, who generously granted me a sabbatical to explore the bizarre world of tornadoes.

Special thanks to Dick Rogers, brainstormer extraordinaire; everyone at the National Severe Storms Laboratory, especially the amiable and admirable Erik Rasmussen; Dane Konop of the National Oceanic and Atmospheric Administration; Dan Pendick of *Earth Magazine;* Rick Gore, my editor at *National Geographic;* the operators of Toronto Science Island, where I discovered meteorology at age ten; and the weather writers who influenced my youth—Paul E. Lehr, R. Will Burnett, Herbert S. Zim, Philip D. Thompson, and Robert O'Brien. Also, a belated thanks to five people who made a difference, each at a crucial moment in my life, but who probably don't know it: Robert Morgan, Jim Squires, June Smith, Will Hearst III, and Paul Freiberger.

Naturally, I alone am responsible for any mistakes herein.

CONTENTS

FOREWORD

Two decades ago, *Jaws* encouraged untold flocks of youngsters to head for libraries or bookstores and ask clerks, "Do you have any books about sharks?" Likewise, *Twister* may stimulate young and old to learn more about tornadoes, the most astounding and frightening of atmospheric phenomena. Hopefully, this book will inspire readers to a wider interest in weather, atmospheric science, and earth science in general. Such interests are especially worth cultivating at a time when the planetary ecosystem is endangered. Earth requires careful cultivation, and the best cultivators are scientifically savvy citizens.

Every filmmaker who portrays a natural disaster—a tornado or a hurricane or an earthquake or a tsunami or a volcanic eruption or a shark attack, or whatever—faces the same basic questions: How can this natural phenomenon, so alien to the ordinary filmgoer's experience, be rendered realistically on the screen? How can the realistic look be balanced with the audience's expectations? (For example, some filmgoers may assume that tornadoes resemble the snaky specter in *The Wizard of Oz,* a specter that was, in fact, closer to folklore than reality.) And how can the film's realism be "charged" for dramatic purposes without sacrificing scientific credibility?

In short, how can the silver screen do justice to the marvels of nature and, thereby, covertly educate moviegoers while overtly entertaining them? It is a daunting task, which can be solved only by an army of talented and passionate artists—from actors to editors and sound engineers to computer experts.

Very few people have gotten a good, close look at a tornado—say, from a distance equivalent to a few city blocks. And almost no one has been *inside* a tornado as it rages overhead. But any filmgoer can now undergo that unparalleled experience, thanks to the recent marriage of high-speed computers and Hollywood filmmakers. *Twister* does for tornadoes what *Jurassic Park* did for dinosaurs: It brings them to life on the screen, in computer-generated images that are virtually indistinguishable from photographic reality. Consequently, every filmgoer has the potential to become a tornado chaser—and without risking her or his life in the process.

Twister dramatizes the work of one of the strangest elites in science: tornado chasers. Hollywood has a long history of portraying scientists as monsters or madmen. In contrast, *Twister* portrays them as humans with recognizable feelings who are driven by genuine curiosity about nature. *Twister* director Jan De Bont—who directed the bomb-on-a-bus thriller *Speed*—wanted actors that the audience could relate to, who not only look like real people but who *act* like them.

That's why Bill Paxton and Helen Hunt struck De Bont as perfect for the lead roles. "From the moment I read the script, I knew whom I wanted: Bill Paxton and Helen Hunt," De Bont says. "It's just intuition; I didn't think about it for a second further." In *Twister,* Hunt and Paxton portray people who are essentially like us, with one glaring difference: They chase tornadoes.

One of Hollywood's emerging major stars, film veteran Paxton won international attention in director Ron Howard's *Apollo 13* as Fred Haise, the symbol of Everyman, the antithesis of macho "Right Stuff" mythology, aboard the stricken spaceship. Audiences instantly empathized with his character, a brave but shivering, sickly, and occasionally defensive astronaut—an ordinary-seeming American embarked on an extraordinary adventure.

In *Twister,* Paxton plays a tornado expert torn between loves—love of chasing, love for his soon-to-be-ex-wife, love for his new fiancée (played by Jami Gertz), and anger at the film's heavy, a former colleague (played by Cary Elwes) whom Paxton accuses of stealing his idea for ejecting sensors into the tornado funnel. Paxton "looks like he's from the countryside. He's born in that region, anyway," De Bont said. "I like actors to *be* what they have to represent."

De Bont's prescription also fits Hunt. She is the female star of the acclaimed TV comedy *Mad About You,* where she portrays an intense but appealingly funny New York woman married to Paul Reiser. "She looks like a real person, like your neighbor. And it was really hard to get her. She had a commitment to the TV series; the studio was afraid she wouldn't finish in time to get her back to the TV series, and what were we going to do if we ran over schedule? . . . We finally had to promise the studio an 'end date' to get her back to NBC. We just barely made it."

In *Twister*, Hunt plays a self-willed woman named Jo Harding, who is driven by a childhood encounter with a tornado to chase and study these bizarre phenomena. Hunt plays the most dynamic female scientist on film in a long time, perhaps ever.

For years, teachers and education experts have complained that it's hard to persuade young girls to pursue scientific careers partly because they see so few role models on TV and in films. Considering its huge potential appeal to young moviegoers, *Twister* is a step toward altering sexist stereotypes about science and adventure. *Twister* "is a movie that has a very strong female role—a woman [Hunt] who is totally in control of herself and her own life," says De Bont (who directed another dynamic female character in his last film—Sandra Bullock, who drove the bus in *Speed).* "She's not dependent on somebody else, and she knows exactly what she wants to do: She wants to chase tornadoes. She wants to create a better warning system for tornadoes so fewer people get hurt. And nobody can stop her. And that's what I like about her."

De Bont shot *Twister* on location in Oklahoma and Iowa, where tornadoes frequently tear across the prairie. Many film crews on location endure bad weather, but *Twister*'s makers were wracked by both bad and *good* weather. Bad weather often caused their heavy equipment to bog down in mud on narrow country roads where it was difficult to turn around. Good weather frequently denied them the storm footage vital for the film.

Twister was "probably five times as difficult as *Speed*," De Bont said. "To be honest, if I had known it was going to be this difficult, I might have thought a second time about doing it.

"It was *so* complex. The equipment we needed was so big, and to be on all these rural roads where you could not turn cars around, and we got stuck. . . . We had terrible weather, too. There was a lot of flooding in Oklahoma. . . . We got stuck in the mud, all the equipment and tractors and bulldozers and cranes, and I thought, 'How do I ever get out of here?' There were hailstorms and thunderstorms *continuously*.

"The noise of all those jet engines and wind machines became a major headache. I lost my voice so many times trying to shout over the sound level of the wind machines, I was forced to use hand signals. For the actors it was hard, too, because when you have those wind machines and jet engines aimed at you, you don't act, you just try to survive! Debris flew in their mouths as they were saying their lines, and they'd gag and have to stop talking."

De Bont is no stranger to rugged filmmaking. Born in Holland, in 1943, he worked as a director of photography, gaining attention for his work with Dutch directors, including Paul Verhoeven. In the United States, he worked on complex, energetic films such as *Die Hard* and *The Hunt for Red October*. In terms of popular renown, his breakthrough film was *Speed*, which introduced a truly mass audience to his flair for threading humor and personalities through complex, high-tech plots.

Despite De Bont's past experience, the pressure involved in making *Twister* was "absolutely horrifying," he says. "The movie was so complex because of all the physical and computer effects. The physical effects on the set were unbelievable. Every day, there're hundreds of people asking you a million questions that will never stop. Our days would start at six in the morning, and my day wouldn't end until ten or eleven in the evening. And we'd be shooting seven days a week."

De Bont hired a meteorologist, Vince Miller, to work with the film crew to alert them to coming weather conditions. De Bont was especially concerned about Midwestern lightning, which is nothing short of spectacular.

"Those bolts were so powerful that when they flashed, it was like daylight—I had never seen anything like that. It was just unbelievable, absolutely beautiful," says Ian Bryce, another *Twister* producer.

Meanwhile, "you've got 200 to 250 people out there, and you're responsible for their lives, and there's no basement you can put all 250 people in.

"This is the hardest movie I've worked on," Bryce affirmed, "and I've worked on a *lot* of [special] effects movies."

The filmmakers simulated a hailstorm by moving seven trucks full of ice down from Milwaukee. The ice had been injected with milk to make it resemble hail. Then crew members shoved 400-pound ice blocks into a chipping machine. The ice fragments were sprayed over the actors at a site they dubbed Hailstorm Hill. While the hail spewed overhead, the crew aimed a 707 jet aircraft engine (mounted on the back of a 48-foot flatbed truck) at the actors. Other crew members tossed branches and other debris into the jet's winds to simulate hurtling tornado debris. It was quite a spectacle.

Producer Kathleen Kennedy said: "We were moving a crew of 250 to 300 people constantly, sometimes three, four, five moves a day. That meant the transportation crews would be up all night long moving trucks, moving base camps, making sure everybody had a place to live during the day.

"It got very, very hot—the Midwest can get 100 percent humidity, 90 degrees. It's pretty rough to be out working in those conditions, day in and day out," Kennedy said.

But it was worth it, added Kennedy, a veteran producer of some of Hollywood's most successful films. "If you want a spiritual experience, you should go spend April to June in the Midwest, because you have never *seen* cloud formations like this! You watch everything in the sky happening in front of you as if you were watching time-lapse photography. We would literally watch cloud towers shoot into the sky and within fifteen minutes one little cloud would rise to become one 30,000 feet high."

John Frazier was in charge of special physical effects. He works in Sunland, California, in a building that, from the outside, looks more like a large auto repair shop than a film fantasy factory. The only external hint that odd stuff goes on within is a large, partly dismantled green dragon in the driveway. (He built the dragon for a ceremony at his daughter's high school.)

Frazier is an easygoing Hollywood veteran who has worked on numerous films as diverse as *Hoffa*, *Speed*, *Apollo 13*, and Jim Carrey's *Cable Guy*. He holds out a box full of what appear to be little spherical gizmos with translucent covers, chromium bottoms, black wires on the outside, and blinking red and green lights on the interior. "We made thousands of these things. Take some." In *Twister*, the balls were scientific sensors that the researchers launch into a tornado.

A movie's physical props, like its digital effects, may contain inside jokes that the audience never sees. The sensors were made by a physical effects worker whose nickname is Fluffy ("because he looks like marshmallow," Frazier explains). Frazier holds up the translucent sphere and points to the name of an imaginary company neatly printed inside the sphere: Flufftronics.

Frazier, along with production designer Joe Nemec, also supervised crews that used bulldozers to tear down a section of an Oklahoma town covering two city blocks. The movie studio purchased all homes and buildings in that area for the film, then ripped them apart to portray the aftermath of a tornado.

Twister's trickiest and riskiest physical effect involved a tractor-trailer that is picked up by a tornado, then dropped in a fiery explosion on the highway. Frazier's crew had to strip down the tractor-trailer until it was light enough to be lifted by a crane. Then two stunt experts, representing Jo and Bill, drove in a Dodge pickup truck toward the tractor-trailer as it dangled 75 feet above the ground. The tractor-trailer was wired with explosives. At a precisely specified moment, Frazier pressed a button to release the tractor-trailer. If his calculations were right, the tractor-trailer would hit the ground about 50 feet in front of the approaching stunt crew. A moment's miscalculation could kill two people. The blast came off without a hitch. That one shot cost at least $100,000.

"You'll wake up at all hours of the night, thinking about how to do a particular effect," Frazier says. He also worries about how to pull off the effect without letting the audience know how it was done. Typically, he has nothing to fear; an audience is usually too dazzled by a physical effect to notice the movie-maker's sleight of hand. At the end of *Speed*, Frazier says, "you can see the cable towing the bus into the airplane. But nobody has ever seen that cable but me."

Twister's setting is as grandiose as its subject: the Midwest, a terrain as rich in myth for Americans as the Aegean is for Greeks. Such a vast setting calls for the right "eye"—the eye of a skilled director of photography.

What makes the Midwestern sky "so interesting is that the terrain is so *flat*—more than half of what you're seeing is sky! So you tend to pay a lot of attention to it," said director of photography Jack Green. "They've got these incredible cloud patterns passing through—clouds that contrast against a clear, intense blue and nearly unpolluted sky."

Green has been in the film business more than forty years. He has worked with major figures such as Clint Eastwood, for whom Green shot (among other films) *Unforgiven*. For *Twister*'s film stock, Green used "very fine-grain film" to make it easy for digital effects artists to add realistic-looking computerized images of tornadoes. (This book's Afterword tells about how the digital effects were done.)

Looking back on his *Twister* experience, Green recalls his and the rest of the film crew's seemingly endless battles with bad Midwestern weather—thunderstorms, lightning, muddy roads. "I think the credit list after this show will be as long as the show," he jokes.

Tornadoes are terrifying partly because they sound so horrible—"like a thousand freight trains," according to a common description. Consequently, one of *Twister*'s most important artists was the sound effects editor, Steve Flick.

As a painter works with paints to make a palette of color, a sound effects expert works with different sounds to create an "emotional palette," Flick said. A simple example is a creaking door in a haunted house. You know what that sound is like; perhaps you can hear it in your mind as you read these words. And if effectively used in a film, that sound produces an emotional reaction (suspense or fear).

For *Twister*, Flick and sound designer John Pospisil searched for sounds with a quality that Flick calls "aggressive strangeness." They listened to recordings of sounds ranging from freight trains and roller-coasters to roaring lions.

To make new and different wind sounds, they constructed a box filled with chicken wire, stuck a microphone inside, and placed it on top of a car. Then they rolled the car downhill—turning the engine off so that it wouldn't interfere with the sound recording.

They also reviewed recordings of camels and noted that these creatures emit sounds that are "wet and lugubrious and nasty—they have a tremendous amount of 'globble' sound to them." As he listened to the camel recordings over and over, Flick turned down the pitch, and the camels' sounds developed a moaning, cavernous quality that, he felt, nicely captured the eerie vastness of a tornado.

Perhaps no film art is simultaneously as subtle and as powerful as editing. The arrangement (and re-arrangement) of pieces of film can make the difference between a mediocre scene and a great one.

The editor on *Twister* is Michael Kahn, one of Hollywood's most distinguished film editors. He began his career working on TV editing for *I Love Lucy* and other shows. He won an Academy Award for his editing on *Raiders of the Lost Ark*, and also worked on films as diverse as *Close Encounters of the Third Kind* and *The Color Purple*. *Twister* was his first opportunity to work with digital editing, in which the entire film is digitized, then stored on a computerized editing machine called Lightworks. The device is bigger than a desk and surrounded by computer disk storage equipment in Kahn's Santa Monica office. He sits in front of the computer screen and watches a digitized copy of the movie unfold on the screen, complete with sound. By manipulating dials, he rearranges frames of the film and does fade-ins, fade-outs, jump cuts, and all the other gimmicks of the film editor's trade—without touching a frame of movie celluloid.

The latter work is reserved for Kahn's assistants.

After he finishes editing the digitized version of the film, he has the computer print out a list indicating exactly how he rearranged it, frame by frame. He gives the list to an aide, who goes to the film vault, removes the necessary copies of the original celluloid footage, and cuts and rearranges it on a traditional editing machine. For Kahn, Lightworks allows him to be as imaginative and clever as he desires, while others handle the laborious "cutting and snipping." The main benefit of Lightworks, he says, is that it's so easy and comfortable for him to use. "The only problem," he adds with a grin, "was that I gained fifteen pounds—I'm just sitting and pushing buttons."

Throughout the editing of *Twister*, Kahn regularly consulted with De Bont and frequently visited the shooting locations in Oklahoma and Iowa. Film school textbooks are full of rules on how to edit a movie, but Kahn seems blissfully antitheoretical. "We used to have more rules than you can shake a stick at. . . . But today I don't think there are any rules. You just do what works . . . what *feels* right."

And he feels that his editing of *Twister* will enhance exactly the emotional effects that De Bont seeks: Thrills. Curiosity. Suspense. Romance. Terror. *Lots* of terror.

CHAPTER 1

Ground Zero

Envision a dark, cylindrical object several times as tall as the Empire State Building, and many times as wide. It plummets from a thundercloud, then screeches and spins across the countryside, with winds far faster than a hurricane's. It buzz-saws homes in half, turns towns into toothpicks, and scatters cattle and people like so much confetti.

When a tornado nears, most sane people flee. But tornado chasers grab their video cameras, board their cars and vans, and race into the countryside, hoping to get as close as possible to the most brutal and baffling of atmospheric phenomena. Most chasers are amateur weather buffs. But a small percentage are scientists, such as the brave souls of the VORTEX tornado-chasing project. Their goal is to understand how tornadoes form and how better to predict them. Better tornado forecasts will be more and more crucial in future decades, for over the next century or two, as the United States population grows and spreads across the countryside, tornadoes may become the most common form of severe natural disaster.

The United States is already the world capital of tornadoes. Tornadoes strike many other countries, but nowhere as ferociously or abundantly as they strike the United States—and not only the Midwest; they even hit Alaska! In 1994, tornadoes killed 69 Americans—the highest yearly tornado death rate since 1984—and injured 1,139. Total damage approached half a billion dollars.

Every spring, a battle ensues in the sky over the midwestern United States. Each day the sun rises a little higher, and as it does it heats the waters of the Gulf of Mexico. Those waters evaporate and creep north into the United States. Somewhere over the plains states, this tongue of warm, humid air encounters cold, dry air left over from winter. Placing warm, moist air beneath cold, dry air is akin to dropping a match into a gas tank: The moisture rises and forms clouds, some of them thunderheads twice the height of Mount Everest. As energetic as many atomic bombs, the ensuing thunderstorms bring lightning, heavy rain, golfball-size hail, and tornadoes to the American heartland.

Since 1953, twisters have killed more than 3,700 Americans, injured tens of thousands more, and wreaked billions of dollars in damage. Their fastest winds approach 300 miles per hour. (By contrast, a hurricane is defined as a storm with winds faster than 74 mph.) A typical tornado is hundreds of feet wide, but some have been wider than a mile. Tornadoes turn bricks, pianos, and railway cars into missiles. They shoot straws into trees, playing cards into metal, wood splinters into steel. For days after a twister, victims may pluck sand, grass, and slivers of glass from their skin.

Tornadoes often strike suddenly and without warning. For more than a century, scientists have struggled to understand how tornadoes form. They have learned much, and today's tornado forecasts are the best ever. Some scientists have driven (deliberately or accidentally) within a hundred feet of tornado funnels. Their hearts pounded as they filmed or videotaped the mad whirlwinds. Incredibly, no funnel has killed a scientist—yet.

The grandest tornado chase in the history of science was VORTEX, or Verification of the Origins of Rotation in Tornadoes Experiment. It lasted two years and involved about 120 scientists, students, and aides from 14 universities and other research institutions.

Ironically, VORTEX almost flopped. For mysterious climatic reasons, Mother Nature created few exciting tornadoes in 1994 and 1995. But in June 1995, days before the project's demise, the scientists hurried to the west Texas plains to witness a tornado of mythic grandeur. Thanks to what they saw and learned, tornado research may never be the same.

The VORTEX field coordinator was Erik N. Rasmussen. Like many VORTEX scientists, Rasmussen began chasing twisters as a teenager. As a meteorology graduate student at Texas Tech in the early 1980s, his weather forecasts amazed everyone. Rasmussen was so prophetic that he became known as the Dryline Kid, in reference to an ever-shifting atmospheric boundary, the dryline, that separates dry air from moist air and often spawns severe storms, including tornadoes. The magazine *Weatherwise* cited Rasmussen's "renowned . . . ability to pick the exact spot a tornado will explode to [the] ground." That sounds like an exaggeration, but it was literally true on at least one shocking occasion. A video camera recorded the incident.

May 1981: It's an exciting week in Tornado Alley; numerous twisters are breaking out all over Oklahoma. A radar unit scans a tornadic storm near the town of Binger in unprecedented detail, revealing its internal structure as an X ray reveals a patient's skeleton. The colorful scientist Stirling Colgate risked death by flying an airplane around a tornado and firing instrumented rockets at it.

Meanwhile, east of Oklahoma City, the twenty-three-year-old Rasmussen and his grad school buddies are driving around the countryside, searching for a twister, any twister. They're carrying a sound-recording device that they plan to drop near the funnel. With luck, the sound measurements could lead to a "tornado alarm"—a sound sensor that rings when it "hears" a twister coming.

The black and white videotape shows what happens next: Driving conditions are rotten on the two-lane road. The windshield streams with rain. Gales buffet the car. "We're heading right into the mesocyclone," Rasmussen declares on the videotape sound track. A mesocyclone is a miles-wide, vertical column of rotating air (like a spinning cylinder) within the thundercloud. The mesocyclone may sprout a much thinner, faster column that descends to the ground—the tornado.

The headlights of another car approach from the opposite direction. Moment by moment, Rasmussen records the fast-changing weather: "Rain, no hail." A bolt of lightning sparks off the road to the left. "CG!" shouts a voice in the car. "CG" means cloud-to-ground lightning. Lightning is the biggest danger, next to the tornado itself.

"Very strong winds, rain and hail, moving very rapidly eastward just ahead of us. Watch for possible debris. We're entering a high danger zone." Rasmussen sounds as cool as Captain Kirk ordering an attack on the Klingons. The driver, Erik's brother, Neal, hunches over the steering wheel and warily guides the car down the rain-slicked road. There's no telling what monsters lurk ahead, concealed by the whipping curtains of water.

"Estimated wind speed: 50 to 60 knots," Rasmussen continues. "Very dark ahead. . . ." Directly in front of them, a brilliant lightning bolt slashes the sky in half. Trees flail in the high winds. At one second past 6:07 P.M., the Dryline Kid commands: "Okay, now be real careful, Neal, slow down. This will be where we drive right into the tornado, so be very, very careful."

A moment passes. Then—inaudibly on the videotape, but all too clear in Rasmussen's memory—someone in the back of the car says: "Look at that flock of birds."

Rasmussen turns to look. The "birds" are chunks of shattered houses hurtling through the air. He yells: *"Debris! Debris! Tornado! Passing right in front of us!"* On the road ahead, the curtains of rain part, and the monster emerges. Everyone in the car gasps, freezes. A white, boiling tube of debris writhes across the road.

Moments later, the curtains of rain close again. The monster disappears into the deluge. Had they driven a few seconds longer, they might all be dead.

[Storm chasing] is one of the last frontiers for meteorology and mankind on earth.
—Storm chaser's comment on World Wide Web's
Storm Chaser Homepage (1995)

The National Severe Storms Laboratory (NSSL) is to tornado chasing what Florida's John F. Kennedy

Space Center is to space exploration. It is located in Norman, Oklahoma, where scientific tornado chasing has been centered since the early 1970s. Norman is an urban speck surrounded by cattle country.

Two odd things happened in Norman in April 1995. At 9:02 A.M. on April 19, at the National Weather Service (NWS) office off Halley Road, the Doppler weather radar detected an unusual event in Oklahoma City, about 20 miles to the north. On the radar screen, a small blob swelled outward, like a balloon filling with air. Then the blob faded. Later, weather forecasters realized to their horror that the blob was an exploding building—the Alfred P. Murrah Federal Building in Oklahoma City, where, on that sunny morning, a terrorist bomb killed more than 160 men, women, and children.

The other odd event also occurred off Halley Road, two days earlier, on April 17. A peculiar-looking armada of cars gathered in the parking lot by NSSL, a two-story, redbrick structure. Scientists milled around on the grass, conferring. The tops of twelve cars bristled with gadgets—wind vanes, temperature and air pressure sensors, and spinning anemometers. Two white vans gleamed with computers and radio gear. In the back of one van was a Doppler radar unit—white, dish-shaped, and as tall as a man. But this radar would look for tornadoes, not terrorists.

Eventually the scientists waved good-bye to each other (for the last time, if events that day went badly). They boarded their vehicles, started the engines, and—as neatly as a funeral procession—crept down Halley Road, turned onto Robinson Street, and accelerated toward the interstate highway. A year after its first campaign had ended in disappointment, VORTEX was on the road again.

In the distance, warm air rose (or convected). As it rose, the air lifted tons and tons of microscopic water vapor molecules. Air pressure drops with altitude; so as the air ascended, it expanded (as a sealed bag of peanuts expands when you drive up into the mountains). As the air expanded, it cooled; and as it cooled, its water vapor condensed into water droplets. These droplets reflected sunlight and became visible as puffy cumulus clouds.

On April 17, Rasmussen rode in one of the vans. He was the field coordinator or FC, the guy who controls all the vehicles' movements by radio. A storm doesn't move in a straight line across the country. Like a giant amoeba, it unpredictably changes shape, surging here and there and sometimes changing direction. Once the VORTEX fleet neared the storm, Rasmussen would tell different teams where to position themselves around the thunderhead. The storm was constantly moving, so they'd pursue it like mosquitoes orbiting a fleeing rhinoceros. He'd regularly check back with them to ask their azimuth—their position relative to the tornado—so that he could plot the twister's path.

The VORTEX scientists' goal was to get as close as possible to tornadoes without dying. A close look was essential to resolve countless puzzles: How do tornadoes form? How fast are their winds? What is their internal structure? Why do only a small fraction of supercells (long-lived thunderstorms) give birth to tornadoes? Why do some tornadoes rage for hours while others dissipate in seconds? How can weather forecasters improve tornado forecasts? In 1994, they had listed seventeen tornado hypotheses they hoped to prove or disprove. By 1995 the list had grown to twenty-two.

Staffers on different vehicles had different tasks. Some launched weather balloons, to measure the wind speed and direction at different heights. (Different wind velocities at different heights create wind shear, which starts columns of air spinning and may spawn tornadoes.) Others recorded the twister (if any appeared) with 16mm movie and video cameras. Their imagery would later be used to estimate the tornado's wind speed and dynamics.

Scientists also scanned storms with a special kind of radar called "Doppler." You've probably heard of Doppler radar in a less exalted context: Police use it to catch speeders. In meteorology, Doppler radar reveals whether atmospheric particles (such as rain) are moving toward or away from the radar. Scientists use Doppler radar to measure the speed and direction of airflow within storms (based on how air blows particles). They've also used portable Doppler units to measure the highest winds in tornadoes (287 miles per hour is the current record). During

VORTEX, two aircraft flew around storms, Doppler-scanning their interior.*

Meanwhile, on the ground, Josh Wurman and Jerry Straka drove around in a van with a portable Doppler radar unit in back. The radar emits a radar beam with a three-centimeter wavelength, which allows it to see through heavy precipitation. As a tornado approached, they would drive off the road, open the back of the van, aim the radar, and scan the funnel and thundercloud. Their radar images show the tornadic funnel rising from the base of the thundercloud almost all the way to its top—a complete body scan, as a doctor might call it.

Straka, thirty-three, has been a meteorology professor at the University of Oklahoma since 1990. He claims to see tornadoes on one out of three chases,

---

* Doppler radar works on this principle: A radar reflection from a moving object shifts in frequency as the object moves toward or away from the radar. If the object approaches the radar, the reflected radar waves compress together, so the radar receiver detects a higher-frequency signal. If the object recedes, the waves spread out, so the radar detects a lower frequency. The nineteenth-century Austrian physicist Christian Doppler demonstrated frequency shift in sound by placing musicians on a train and having the train move back and forth at high speed. As the train approached, the instruments' acoustic waves rose in pitch. As the train retreated, the pitch lowered. Likewise, when you stand next to the train tracks and a train approaches, its whistle rises in frequency or pitch. As it passes, the pitch falls to a moan.

a remarkably high rate. (The much older and more experienced Professor Howard Bluestein claims only one in seven.)

Straka says, "I was *born* to do this. I've been interested in weather ever since I was young." Straka grew up in Wisconsin, near Milwaukee. His father drove him around the countryside so he could watch storms in action, and "I made my own little forecast every day." He recalls his first tornado: "There was a tornado watch. I went up on my roof, and a tornado passed almost exactly a mile from my house. It was hailing and raining on me."

One of VORTEX's most dangerous tasks involved "turtles." These are low, flat gadgets (hence the name) designed so that they won't flip over in high winds. They contain weather instruments. If a tornado loomed, brave staffers would race ahead of the twister and drop turtles along its likely path. With any luck, the tornado would pass directly over a turtle. If so, its instruments would measure the air-pressure drop within the funnel.

Until VORTEX, no one had ever obtained a convincing measurement of the air pressure within a funnel. The funnel is a rapidly rising, spinning column of air, and as it spins it centrifuges air outward, leaving a slight vacuum behind; thus the pressure drops. The lower the pressure drops in the funnel, the faster it sucks in new air through the bottom (where the centrifuging of air is reduced by friction with the ground) and the faster the funnel rotates. (It's like water going down a drain, except upward).

In 1995, a tornado passed directly over a turtle for the first time.

Initially a tornado is invisible. You may see a spinning cloud of dust on the ground, but no funnel. The funnel appears only if its air pressure drops so low that inrushing air expands and cools enough to condense its water vapor into mist. The mist sheathes the cloud in a neat white column, peppered with whirling black rubble.

On April 17, storms brewed in north Texas. Thunderheads surged over the Red River and into Oklahoma. Inside his van, Rasmussen looked at his computer and studied weather maps and space photos, which he had downloaded by radio from NSSL and NWS. He concluded tornadoes were most likely to form that day near Temple, Oklahoma, just north of the Texas border. So the Dryline Kid ordered the VORTEX fleet to head toward Temple.

Along the road, on this and other VORTEX missions, Rasmussen kept noticing the same sight, a sight that has become painfully apparent over the years. Up and down the highway, everywhere he looked, were storm chasers—hundreds of them. He had mixed feelings on seeing them.

On the one hand, he was once one of them. Rasmussen spent the first twenty years of his life in Hutchinson, a town along the Arkansas River in central Kansas, where "you can't ignore the weather," he said. "I became a weather buff when I was little. I think it was in the second grade when the teacher had us put the forecast and the high- and low-pressure cells on a chart up on the wall. So I started watching the weather. . . . By junior high, I was *really* interested in storms. I would climb a ladder up to the roof to watch them every time they started coming in. By high school, when I had my driver's license, I think one of the first things I did was to drive out and look at storms." He witnessed his first tornado in 1978. "I'd go out to the High Plains with the winds screaming and a huge CB [cumulonimbus or thundercloud] sitting there rotating, hailstorms coming down and popping you on the back of the head. . . . That was really fun.

"I think in the early days of chasing, there was this hunt-like aspect: You'd make your forecast, you'd go out to the blue skies just expecting to see something, and lo and behold, these rock-hard clouds would start building up and growing explosively. And slowly but surely, the storm would start to rotate, and a wall cloud would form, and then your tornado forms . . . and you're sitting out there in the middle of nowhere—you don't even know if there's any other humanity within miles—watching a tornado as the wind whistles through the wires and the birds are singing. That was really something. You'd gone on the hunt, and you'd got your prey, and you had captured it, and you were the *only* one to do it. That was really cool.

"But now," he says, sighing with a trace of resentment, "you drive out to a storm, and there's this *parking lot* out on the highway, with all these people with antennas sticking every which way off their cars and satellite dishes, and it's just . . . *aaahh!* Forget it!" He waves his hand in disgust.

Some scientists criticize the recklessness of a few amateurs—that is, those who drive at 80 mph through a school zone, or cheer "Go baby go!" as a twister shreds a trailer park. "I try to distance myself from the amateurs," says NSSL's Robert Davies-Jones, one of the few chasers with white hair. In his soft English accent, he complains, "There's a fringe element that's just plain irresponsible. Most of them are responsible people, but there's an odd one or two who go around roadblocks, drive across farmers' fields, do crazy things."

By common agreement, the dumbest thing that a chaser can do is to "core punch." Core punching is the equivalent of strolling into a bear's cave with a bag of marshmallows. A chaser core punches by driving through severe rain and hail to get to the other, rain-free side of the storm, where the tornado usually forms. The danger is that you'll be so blinded by rain and hail that you won't see the twister until it lands on top of you.

Yet core punching appears to be an unofficial rite of passage for storm chasers, both scientists and amateurs. Everyone denounces it, yet everyone seems to have done it at one time or another. For every experienced chaser has faced at least one moment when he realizes: I'm going to lose this fast-moving storm if I don't take a shortcut. Unfortunately, the shortcut may lead through the storm core.

"Anyone who says they go chasing purely for science is lying," explains Straka, another ex-amateur-turned-scientist. "During a chase, when you see the expression on their face, you _know_ what's driving them. . . . A lot of people I know dream about tornadoes all the time."

Now in his early fifties, Davies-Jones, one of the world's premier chasers, is expected to set an example for his youthful colleagues. He seems unusually dour for a chaser. Over a quarter of a century, he has witnessed enough twister mayhem to sober the craziest thrill-seeker.

On April 17, as the VORTEX caravan rolled west, the sun continued to shine, heating the terrain and inciting more convection. A few cumuli swelled into towering cumulus congestus clouds, which resembled aerial ski slopes. And some boiled into thunderclouds, whose crystalline tops brushed the sky's "ceiling"—the tropopause, gateway to the stratosphere. Their broad bottoms were as black as night. And if the scientists were lucky, those bottoms would soon bristle with twisters.

Davies-Jones and his team rode in Probe One of the VORTEX fleet. As Probe One neared its destination—Temple, Oklahoma—Davies-Jones's heart soared at the sight of a "glorious supercell" on the horizon.

Then his car broke down. The driver pulled to the side of the road. Davies-Jones used his cellular phone to summon a tow truck. Then they waited . . . and waited . . . and waited. Meanwhile, Rasmussen and the other scientists drove on to Temple. As minutes passed, Davies-Jones listened on his radio to their crackling voices as they approached the Oklahoma-Texas border. They began to sound excited, confused, frightened. Something big was cooking near Temple.

Something big, indeed. "At one point," Rasmussen recalls, "we were just southeast of the reported radar location of the mesocyclone, by about five miles." (Again, a mesocyclone is a rotating, vertical column of air, typically a few miles wide, within a thunderstorm. Tornadoes may descend from a mesocyclone.)

"We were looking northwest, and we saw this big, low-hanging cloud draped down to the south and southwest. It looked like a gust front—cold air outflow from the storm. Looking at the map, I could tell that one road option was to go north in front of this gust front and then go east and stay just right ahead of the storm." That might be risky: A mean gust front can knock a car off the road.

"The other road option went southeast and east, and I knew that if we took that, we would have lost the storm and never caught it again. And it was really the only storm out there; it was moving fairly quickly, and we had to keep jumping to keep up with it.

"So I made the decision to go north and east, thinking that we'd probably end up slicing through this gust front and then coming out ahead of it

Joe Shoulak

1 Rising warm air condenses and forms bumpy mammatocumulus clouds under the thundercloud's "anvil."

2 High-speed winds freeze water vapor, creating wispy, crystalline cirrus clouds atop the storm's "anvil."

3 Wall cloud.

4 Tornado.

5 Rain causes cold downdraft that either (a) snuffs out the mesocyclone tornado or (b) generates its own low-level wind shear, forming a new tornado.

again. We'd encounter some gusty winds and a little battering, but nothing real *hazardous*.

"So we started heading north in a pretty tight group, maybe 100 yards between each car. All of a sudden people starting yelling on the radio that there's a tornado. I'm looking all around and see no tornado. I'm thinking, 'What are they talking about?'" He yelled into his radio microphone: "*Somebody* tell me what they're talking about!"

"Then the people in *my* car started yelling, 'There's a tornado, there's a tornado!'" He looked around again, still saw nothing, and barked: "*Will you people tell me what you're talking about!?*

"And all of a sudden, about 100 meters west of us in the field, I see this dust whirl start to form—a real tight little one. I thought: 'It's *right here*.' They should have been yelling: 'There's a funnel *overhead.*'

"I knew the tornado would be moving roughly east. So I got on the radio, and I yelled, '*Tornado just west of the road. The vehicles in front of the FC [Rasmussen] should go north as fast as you can. Vehicles behind FC, stop now and let the tornado cross road in front of you.*' That would make a 'hole' in the caravan for the tornado to go through.

"I jumped up in my seat and watched out the back window as the tornado crossed the road. I was just freaked because the vehicle behind me was a group that liked to stay with me. They felt insecure if they weren't right on my bumper. So they didn't follow my instructions; they decided to go ahead and follow us down the road. I saw this tornado coming at their vehicle, and I thought: *'It's going to take them out.'*"

The twister ripped across the road. An explosion of dust and debris blocked Rasmussen's view of the car behind him.

In another car, Straka watched the tornado approach the road. The funnel was small but furious. He was sure it would hit some cars, "and that would be the end of VORTEX." By radio to Rasmussen, Straka read off the distances between the twister and the rear car: "100 feet . . . 50 feet . . ." The funnel passed within a stone's throw of the rear car's bumper. Straka shouted into his mike: "No cars in the air!"

That type of close call frayed Rasmussen's nerves. And the chase season was just beginning; what would the rest of the season bring?

Miles away, Davies-Jones and his team fumed by their dead sedan. They had spent hours waiting for the tow truck. Tumbleweeds jiggled across the prairie. Cars whizzed by indifferently.

Finally the tow truck arrived. After their vehicle was repaired, Davies-Jones and crew glumly drove toward a motel, figuring they had missed all the fun.

But not quite. "Near dark," he recalls, "this other line of thunderstorms developed to our west, and Bill, my driver, said: 'Boy, that looks like a wall cloud, if I didn't know any better.' It turned out it *was* a wall cloud, headed right toward us. It passed just to our north.

"This wind starts blowing about 70 mph, and each gust seemed to be higher than the one before it." Visibility fell to zero. "I really thought about getting out of the car and hitting the ditch because I thought our car was going to be blown across the road."

They never saw any tornado, and the turmoil lasted just a minute. "A scary minute." The brief blast lifted their spirits, and they continued to a motel, tired but happy.

By the start of June 1995, days before VORTEX's scheduled shutdown, "we didn't have a whole lot of very exciting data," Davies-Jones admits. It looked as if the project would end—its final day was June 15—with little to show for everyone's toil. By early June, the VORTEX scientists were wearing out. VORTEX scientist John T. Snow of the University of Oklahoma grew worried about the researchers' "sleep deprivation [and] accumulated fatigue. They had gone on for, I guess, ten weeks by that time."

On the evening of June 1, Rasmussen studied the weather charts and concluded that storms would soon be brewing over Clovis, New Mexico. Clovis was 100 miles northwest of Lubbock, Texas, where he had attended Texas Tech in the early 1980s. "I looked at the forecast for the Lubbock winds, and they were forecast to be out of the southeast at 30 mph and unstable. I thought, 'Wow, when I lived there, that always meant big stuff.' So I was excited the night before.

"I came in next morning. Nothing had changed much. It still looked like there was going to be this strong, low-level southeast wind and big instability, and I thought, 'It looks like [we'll have] a really typical west Texas tornado outbreak.'

"Sure enough, we got down to west Texas, almost to Clovis, and these *big, hard* clouds were going up in eastern New Mexico!" The clouds resembled mountains of whipped cream. The higher they rose, the darker their bases became. Their tops soon bumped against the tropopause. At those ethereal heights, cold, high-speed winds froze the clouds' water vapor into ice crystals and fanned them outward, forming classic thunderhead "anvils."

Time passed; the thunderheads evolved very slowly. Rasmussen grew antsy. Why weren't the thunderheads turning into thunderstorms? "It made me angry."

Eventually a few storms intensified, especially one near Clovis, "and we started following it northeastward. . . . The inflow wind got so strong and the dust got so thick that we couldn't see the cars in front of us. Some of the power lines were being torn down. I thought, 'No matter what we see today, it's going be something exciting, because you don't get that kind of inflow wind on an average storm.'

"Shortly thereafter, we started getting reports of very intense rotation on the Doppler radar. Jerry called in from the mobile Doppler and said he'd seen all kinds of folds in the wind velocity. That means the velocity is stronger than what the radar resolves. When that happens, you know the storm is getting stronger and stronger. Also, Probe One and a few other Probes started reporting strong rotation and a bit of blowing dust."

The real action began just southwest of the small Texas panhandle town of Friona, about 30 miles northeast of Clovis. A violent twister formed southwest of the town, passed on the southern outskirts and through the eastern side of the community. It destroyed a large grain elevator and wrecked the local airport, including a large steel building. "The anchor bolts holding the columns of this building were ripped out of the concrete slab, with part of the slab going with the bolts," Rasmussen and Straka said. "The heavy beams were left in a twisted heap. One I-beam became a missile and was thrown about 100 meters." The tornado picked up a railroad boxcar weighing several tons and bounced it for 100 meters through a cemetery, smashing monuments and digging a two-foot-deep hole into an asphalt road. Then the Friona tornado disappeared into heavy rain. Throughout the storm, the VORTEX vehicles raced around the twister, scanning it with Doppler radar, dropping turtles, and launching unmanned balloons with weather instruments and radio transmitters.

"There were at least six rotating supercells in a three-county area," Rasmussen recalls. "The sky was almost black as night. Blowing dust everywhere. I felt like the atmosphere had gone completely berserk."

Then he got a radio report that yet another storm was forming 20 miles to the east, near a flyspeck of a town called Dimmitt. He ordered his team to head there. He felt both happy and unhappy: happy because at Friona, they had finally cornered a big tornado; unhappy "because I knew we hadn't gotten real comprehensive data" there. Dimmitt offered a second chance.

"We get down to Dimmitt, turn east, and here's this big supercell bearing down on the town with a big rotating updraft." He observed a "clear slot," an opening in the storm caused by descending drier air. He got on the radio and announced that he expected to see "a significant tornado in the next few minutes." The Dryline Kid was right again: Soon a fat funnel cloud began to descend.

The tornado hit the south side of Dimmitt. It crossed State Road 86 and ripped off hundreds of square meters of road and spewed the black asphalt more than 600 feet into a field. Two truck-trailers were blown away.

Rasmussen was 6 miles east of Dimmitt. He had a beautiful view of the tornado. He tried to radio to his troops who were closer to the storm. He tried and tried. No one answered. They were watching the tornado.

"What happened at Dimmitt was that the tornado formed and"—Rasmussen's voice softens, his eyes get a faraway look—"everybody was just *mesmer-*

ized. I mean, it was a *beautiful* sight. And for about 40 seconds, I couldn't get anybody to tell me what the azimuth of the tornado was from their vehicle. . . . No one would tell me anything."

That was too much for Rasmussen. After two years of repeated frustration, here they were, within the equivalent of a few city blocks of the mother of all VORTEX tornadoes, and he couldn't get anyone to pick up their blasted microphones. He gleefully imitates the tantrum he threw—yelling, fists smacking the roof—as this greatest of VORTEX twisters roared by.

As it turned out, Dimmitt was a historic tornado. It was the first major twister that VORTEX scientists documented from beginning to end. Radar probed its innards in unprecedented detail; movie film and videotape recorded its mad whirrings.

For years to come, the scientists will pore over the Dimmitt data and plumb its secrets. It will be used to test theories of twister formation and, perhaps, to find better ways to forecast them. VORTEX, which could have ended in failure, climaxed in triumph at Dimmitt, where even the coolest scientists momentarily forgot themselves and, jaws hanging and arms limp, gazed in awe at the whirling leviathan. "Beautiful," they whispered to themselves, over and over and over. And beautiful it was—as beautiful, in its own way, as the Grand Canyon or a solar eclipse.

Enraptured by this aerial vision, anyone might forget what a tornado really is: an engine of annihilation that can wipe a town from the face of the Earth. Literally.

CHAPTER 2

A World Destroyed

*A*fter midnight on June 8, 1984, a twister demolished the sleeping village of Barneveld, Wisconsin. Virtually nothing was left standing. Some residents thought a nuclear bomb had fallen. The death toll of nine was small as major tornadoes go. Yet Barneveld was so tiny, its obliteration so total, and its people such evocative symbols of an American ideal—small town life, far from the pressures and alienation of the city—that its fate made global headlines.

The Barneveld disaster is scientifically important because it inspired a new area of tornado research, long-distance debris dispersal. The tornado blew debris for extraordinary distances, so extraordinary that it raised an unsettling question: What would happen if a tornado hit a chemical plant, radioactive waste site, or other environmentally sensitive facility and scattered its toxins for tens or hundreds of miles?

The tragedy also shattered one of the commonest American delusions about tornadoes: that a town can be protected from twisters by a local quirk of topography. Barnevelders regarded a local hillside as their shield against tornadoes—a paper shield, as it turned out. Across America today, residents of countless other communities suffer similar delusions of immunity from the atmosphere's cruelest storm. If history is any guide, there is only one cure for this delusion: a visit from a tornado. Its visit exacts not only a physical price, but a psychological one. After the winds subside, townspeople may rebuild their homes and businesses and schools. But to survivors, the sky may never look so blue and vast and hopeful again; they may perceive a dark lining in every silver cloud.

If you drive west from Madison, Wisconsin, on Highway 18-151, you pass through farm country. Tractors plow fields; cows meander; a white, spotted horse looks sleepily out of a stall. Just past the sign for Lost River Cave, turn right on the "K" road, pass the old cemetery, and you're in Barneveld.

Long ago, on spring and summer evenings, songbirds chirped in Barneveld's century-old oak trees as the shadows grew long. On Jenniton Avenue lived Mary Ann Myers, a petite, cheerful-looking widow with her white hair in a bun. She liked to sit outside in the evening and watch the western horizon. There, incoming thunderstorms flickered with lightning. Immense cold fronts surged out of Canada or the Rockies and passed over southern Wisconsin en route to the Great Lakes, where they occasionally spawned waterspouts before drenching Chicago and points east.

June 7, 1984, was "a hot sticky night, a real true summer night," Mary Ann recalls. To the west, in Iowa on the other side of the Mississippi River, storms were churning and tornadoes touched down. Mary Ann had to travel to a wedding the next day, so she stayed up late that night paying bills, balancing her checkbook, and writing notes to her family. Nowadays, she wonders if she did all those things because she had a "premonition" of coming events. Anyway, she penned the last note and went to bed. Also sleeping in her two-story duplex were her two daughters, Anita and Jill, Anita's son, Joey, and the elderly mother of Mary Ann's late husband. Usually Anita put four-month-old Joey in his crib at bedtime. But that night, for some reason, Anita took Joey to bed with her.

The lights winked out across Barneveld. Anita Jabs, who ran the local store with her husband, Ron, had heard about the Iowa tornadoes and watched TV until 11:00 P.M., waiting for a tornado warning. None came. So she hit the sack. Elsewhere in town, two young parents, Charles and Susan Aschliman, tucked their two-year-old boy, Matthew, into bed. After a day spent planting flowers in their garden, Roger and Jeanne Jabs turned out the lights; the only sounds in the house were the panting of their dog, Belle, and the purring of the cat, Kalamazoo. Over in Barneveld's handsome new Thoni subdivision, James Slewitzke prepared for bed. A resident of northern Wisconsin, he was visiting Barneveld to help his sister Elaine paint her house.

Sometime after midnight, 30 miles southwest of Barneveld, a tornado touched down near the village of Belmont. It was a small twister—an "F2" tornado, about 120 feet wide. ("F2" represents a "significant" tornado on the Fujita Scale, which investigators use to estimate the intensity of tornadoes based mainly on building damage.) The Belmont twister was the first of several tornadoes that would whir across southern Wisconsin in the next hour or so.

At 12:50 A.M.—that's when everyone's electric clocks stopped—a "horrendous wind" awoke Anita Jabs. She turned over in bed and punched her husband, Ron. "I'm going to the basement," she snapped. "You get Jason and I'll get the girls."

At Jeanne Jabs's home, she left bed to close a window. Then the wall disintegrated. She seized her cat, Kalamazoo, and hid behind a chair.

A spectacular blast of lightning awoke Mary Ann Myers. She ran to her bedroom door to tell her family to hurry to the basement. She opened the door—

and stopped dead in her tracks. The other side of the house was gone.

"I was looking outside at the ginkgo tree, blowing in the wind. . . . I died a little then," she recalls. "I couldn't breathe—I wonder if it was the shock or the air pressure. I remember screaming. I had two daughters and a grandson on the other side of the house, and a mother-in-law down below, and I told myself: 'They aren't there anymore.' I screamed and prayed to God, all at the same time."

Numerous other Barnevelders were blown from their homes. One second they were fast asleep, warm under the covers while rain drilled the roof and winds shook the windowpanes. The next second they awoke in their pajamas, sprawled in a muddy field hundreds of feet from their beds. They felt wet. Were they soaked by the rain? Or bleeding to death? They couldn't tell; the gale had knocked out every light in town.

In the ruins of Mary Ann Myers's duplex, she quivered and sobbed for her lost loved ones. "I really thought they were gone. I thought: What am I going to do? I'd lost my husband to cancer several years before. I thought, 'I can't handle this.' "

Then she heard their voices. They had survived. The wind had blown Anita, Joey, Jill, and her mother-in-law into the yard. Tiny Joey was seriously injured but alive. Later they would find his crib, smashed flat. He'd have died if Anita had left him in the crib instead of taking him to bed.

Twenty-five miles away in Madison, reporter Ron Seely of the *Wisconsin State Journal* slept in his

Madison home. His phone rang. It was his night city editor, who said something big had happened in Barneveld: A tornado might have hit one or two farms. Seely should check it out. He dressed and headed to the car. "It was ugly out. It looked like a tornado night . . . low, rolling clouds." Seely and the newspaper photographer, Roger Turner, rendezvoused and drove in one car toward Barneveld.

Outside Barneveld, Seely and Turner parked and walked across a field into the village. Seely was puzzled by huge, twisted steel balls in the field. Later he learned they were farm machinery. "Then we got to Main Street in Barneveld, and there was just *nothing*—all you could see was foundations and debris. It was a physical shock to see it."

Smashed glass glistened in the streets. Bedsheets dangled from trees. A fork protruded from the brick wall of the firehouse. Dead songbirds lay on the ground, completely stripped of their feathers. Old Christmas decorations sparkled in the road.

Through the rainy night, search teams prowled the streets, yelling and waving flashlights as they looked for survivors. At dawn, Seely recalled, "Everybody stopped and looked around, and nobody said a thing." The county coroner "pointed to where the bodies had been discovered. There and there and there, he said." The toll: 9 dead, 200 injured, some 160 buildings leveled—90 percent of the town.

The village looked ashen, as if drained of color. In the distance, a farmer on a tractor plowed fields that, to Seely, looked unbelievably green.

"**T**he most powerful tornado ever recorded in Wisconsin in the past 140 years" had flattened Barneveld, said meteorology professor Charles E. Anderson of the University of Wisconsin. The Barneveld funnel carved a 36-mile path across the state, passing within 10 miles of 200,000-population Madison. It was the worst of 26 tornadoes in a multistate outbreak.

> *When people have been through [a tornado], the psychological effect is severe; their lives are altered forever.*
>
> —Ken Wilk of NSSL (1982)

A tornado injures the mind as well as the body. Humans rarely encounter anything else so horrific, short of a wartime blitzkrieg. Psychological damage is inevitable, at least in the short term. The psychic pain is worsened by the twister's creepier pranks. Several weeks after the Barneveld tornado, one resident noticed a curious swelling on his neck. It turned out that an inch-long fragment of glass, probably from a lightbulb, was embedded under his skin. The tornado had turned blades of grass and other debris into miniature bullets, which people plucked out of their flesh for days or months afterward. Later that year, one man coughed up a handful of sand.

After a tornado, a common fear is: Will another one hit soon? Through mid-June, Wisconsin police checked out numerous reports of funnel clouds and twister touchdowns. People fled to their basements at the first rumble of thunder. Civil defense sirens wailed for days. Many funnel reports were probably mistakes. Still, the likelihood of a second hit, while extremely small, is not infinitesimal. For example, in 1948, Tinker Air Force Base in Oklahoma was severely damaged by two tornadoes, five days apart. A church in Guy, Arkansas, has been hit by three separate tornadoes.

A month after the tragedy in Barneveld, "passing storms still cause children to cry and seek the comfort of their parents," the *State Journal* reported. "Many adults who were trapped in their basements complain of being uncomfortable when left alone in a room." Years would pass before they ceased watching dark, wet skies with anxiety; and some have never stopped doing so.

Green Lake is a town about 75 miles northeast of Barneveld. In the second half of 1984, drivers in Green Lake began to have an unusual number of flat tires. They found nails sticking from their tires.

Meanwhile, surprising letters and packages began arriving at the Barneveld post office. The letters and packages contained canceled checks that bore the names of Barneveld residents, photos of Barneveld residents, records from the Barneveld bank, and other Barneveld-related items. People in towns many miles away (some on the other side of the state) had found the items in their yards. The debris had fallen from the sky, from the winds of the same storm that caused the Barneveld tornado. The debris included countless nails, perhaps ripped from the walls of someone's home.

Word of the far-flung debris reached Professor Charles E. Anderson at the University of Wisconsin in Madison. Anderson was a sixty-five-year-old meteorologist and professor of space science and engineering. He had received his Ph.D. in meteorology at MIT, becoming the first African American to win a doctorate in that subject. During World War II he was a captain in the U.S. Army Air Force and a weather forecaster for the legendary all-black Tuskegee Airmen Regiment.

Anderson ran newspaper ads asking the public to report mysterious debris. The ads triggered more than 200 tips from across the state. The tornado had blown away a recreational vehicle; its bumper and license plate were found in Lodi, almost 30 miles from Barneveld. The tornado removed a driver's license from a man's wallet and hurled it to Appleton on the other side of the state. (The wallet remained in Barneveld.)

Anderson's Barneveld study inspired a new branch of tornado science: long-distance debris dispersal, which was later an important part of the VORTEX project. Debris dispersal isn't merely of theoretical interest; it has important practical implications, as shown by Anderson's successor, John T. Snow of the University of Oklahoma.

In 1994 and 1995, Snow and his students followed Anderson's example by running ads asking people to report mysterious debris. They also opened a toll-free telephone line. After tips started to come in, Snow sent his graduate students out in the field to recover debris after tornadoes. Then they sifted through debris and traced much of it back to its place of origin. For example, they traced photos by sending copies to people in communities hit by tornadoes. An accompanying letter asked: Do you recognize anyone in this photo? "People have said, 'Oh yes, that's my granddaughter' and 'That's my high school picture.'" His students traced the origins of debris as diverse as a golf course flag, including part of the plastic pole (which flew 43 miles), a telephone directory (56 miles), and fiberglass roof fragments (about 31 miles). They also traced a man's jacket back to its owner, 40 miles from where it landed. "It had his name monogrammed on it."

Most tornado debris falls to the left of the storm path. Why? Presumably the debris rises into the storm and is swept around by the mesocyclone, and some is ejected toward the north (left). A minority of debris falls to the right, however.

Based on the historical record, researchers have always assumed that long-distance debris dispersal was rare. Only the strongest tornadoes would blow debris for tens or hundreds of miles, they thought. Thomas P. Grazulis, a leading tornado historian, reviewed 13,000 tornado reports from 1871 to 1990 and found only 121 cases with evidence that debris traveled more than 5 miles. Tornadoes have blown chickens and a carton of deer hides 6 miles, a cow and an airplane wing 10 miles, a jar of pickles 18 miles, dead ducks 25 miles, a music box 35 miles, a necktie rack 40 miles, and a wedding gown 50 miles. The record distance is 210 miles, traveled by a canceled check during the Great Bend, Kansas, twister of 1915. This storm destroyed 160 homes and killed 2 people and 1,000 sheep; "hundreds of dead ducks fell from the sky," Grazulis notes.

But Snow's research indicates that long-distance dispersal is remarkably common. During VORTEX, Snow's team collected "reports from 17 separate [tornadoes] . . . over 2 years." That rate hints that long-distance dispersal is "almost 12 times more [common] than what the historical record would suggest."

More important, the Snow team realized that even "moderate" tornadoes can blow debris great distances. An F2 twister struck Moberly, Missouri, on July 4, 1995. It hurled unopened cans of soda 87 miles and a brick (which weighed several pounds) roughly 28 miles.

Now, a decade after the devastation, Barneveld is rebuilt, all shiny and new. The population, which fell to 500 or so after the twister, is now higher than ever, around 850. A half-finished housing complex sprouts on the edge of town. The market and gas station are bigger and more modern-looking than ever. The rustic architecture of yesteryear has disappeared, and taken with it a tactile sense of connection to the past, to those deep familial roots that stretch back to Norway and Germany and Ireland and Sweden.

On the edge of town, a small park has a concrete public memorial, where a plaque lists the victims of the tornado. The plaque vaguely acknowledges "the power of people helping people." The memorial is the only structure in town that looks run-down, as if untended—as if most people would rather forget what happened.

Forgetting is hard, though. Ghosts are everywhere. For years after the tornado, Reverend Twiton cried when he recalled one victim—"little eight-year-old Cassie. She was my friend. She used to come over and visit while I was working on the church's garden. She used to come to church and sit all alone in the front row. I'd look down and there would be Cassie."

Mary Ann Myers's grandson, Joey, spent months in therapy learning how to walk. Today he is twelve, takes medication for seizures, and is a "special needs" child with the mental level, for most cognitive tasks, of a three- or four-year-old. She proudly shows a photo of him. He has big, dark eyes and a soft smile. "He's a beautiful little boy," she said. "If he came in that door now, he'd say, 'Hi Grandma, I love you,' and give me a big hug."

But on spring or summer evenings, when thunderheads jam the horizon and sparkle with lightning, Mary Ann Myers no longer sits outside to enjoy the show. She stays indoors.

CHAPTER 3

American Gothic

*A*mericans' battle against tornadoes began more than a century ago. Settlers of the American West encountered terrifying twisters, so terrifying that a few feared the West would prove uninhabitable. However, the modern age of tornado science didn't begin until the 1940s and 1950s, when twisters began to annoy a particularly prickly target: the U.S. military, which launched a tornado-forecasting project. The U.S. Weather Bureau followed suit as the nation urbanized and tornadoes began to clobber fair-size towns.

The earliest colonial record of a possible tornado dates from July 5, 1643. The Massachusetts governor noted in his diary that a "sudden gust" had wrecked a meeting house and blown over a tree, killing a Native American. However, Thomas P. Grazulis, the tornado historian who did climatological research under contract to the Nuclear Regulatory Commission, suspects the 1643 tornado was actually "a gust front or downburst-type storm." It's an early example of a persistent historical puzzle: When is a tornado not a tornado? Our ancestors (particularly early newspaper writers) tended to use the words *tornado, waterspout, cyclone,* and *hurricane* interchangeably.

The "first confirmed true tornado" struck on July 8, 1680, at Cambridge, Massachusetts, Grazulis says. The funnel killed a servant and unroofed a barn. Two years later, a twister ravaged a forest near New Haven, Connecticut. "Great limbs were carried like feathers," a chronicler wrote. Over the next century (which climaxed with the American Revolution), only 17 tornadoes were recorded. The scarcity of eighteenth-century tornado reports reflects the demography of those times: The colonial population was small and restricted largely to the northern part of the Atlantic coast. Few tornadoes were seen because there were few witnesses to see them.

In the next century, white settlers flooded into the nation's interior. They crossed over the Appalachian Mountains and settled in the lush croplands of the Mississippi River, or on the windswept plains teeming with buffalo. There they encountered many hardships: starvation, sickness, bloody conflicts with the natives. But their harshest foe was the sky. Blizzards entombed cattle and cattlemen under snowdrifts; lightning sparked vast prairie fires; drought desiccated a farmer's crops, then hail smashed them flat.

In June 1814, the naturalist John James Audubon saw a tornado near Shawneetown, Illinois.

> Two minutes had scarcely elapsed [since observing a yellowish oval spot toward the southwest] when the whole forest before me was in fearful motion. I saw, to my great astonishment, that the noblest trees of the forest bent their lofty heads for a while, and, unable to stand against the blast, were falling into pieces. . . . [Tree branches] whirled onward like a cloud of feathers. The horrible noise resembled that of the great cataracts of Niagara, and it howled along in the track of the desolating tempest.

Native Americans had settled the continent many millennia earlier. They were no strangers to atmospheric vortices ranging from dust devils to tornadoes.

The Crow tribe told of a boy, Bear White Child, who is picked up by a singing black cloud, then returned to the ground. In prehistoric Kansas, a twister ravaged the Potawatomi tribe. Survivors buried the dead on a hill later named Burnett's Mound, southwest of the future city of Topeka. The natives recounted the disaster in a song that lamented: "The grass is moving, the trees are moving, the whole Earth is moving."

Stereoscopic photos of tornado damage were a Victorian novelty. Stereoscopic photos are near-twin images of the same scene that, when viewed through special eyeglasses, acquire a 3-D quality. They were a popular form of Victorian home entertainment. Hundreds of different stereoscopic images of tornado wreckage were mass-reproduced and sold. They were the tornado videos of their day.

People living in an age before atomic bombs, terrorist explosions, and 747 crashes struggled to describe the violence they had just witnessed. Nothing in their experience, not even the Civil War, could match the apocalyptic sights of a tornado strike. Their accounts bordered on the biblical: "The earth trembled as with an earthquake. The air was filled with sulphurous fumes. Vast waterspouts gyrated to every point of the compass. A roar like Niagara Falls filled the stricken people with fear. The shrieks of the wounded and the wails of the bereaved blanched the faces of the stoutest."

Hope was coming, however, in the emerging science of meteorology.

Anyone who watches a TV weather show knows two facts that early Americans didn't: (1) Storms move horizontally across the Earth, and (2) many storms rotate.

Before the American Revolution, scientists assumed that weather was a local phenomenon. A storm formed in a particular region, then died there. This provincial view of weather was rejected by a man who revolutionized both science and politics.

In Philadelphia on October 21, 1743, Benjamin Franklin looked forward to watching a lunar eclipse. But a storm struck, spoiling the view. Several days later, he read in out-of-town newspapers that residents of Boston (250 miles to the northeast) had seen the eclipse, then endured a violent storm the next day. Was it the same storm that struck Philadelphia on October 21? Franklin concluded it was. Weather moves!

Later scientists realized that American storms typically move from the western half of the compass to the eastern half (usually from southwest to northeast). This discovery suggested a way to forecast the weather: Find out what weather conditions are like to the west.

Unfortunately, the storms moved faster than eighteenth-century communications. By the time Easterners got wind of western storms, the storms had come and gone.

The electric telegraph changed everything. Pioneered by Samuel F. B. Morse and others in the 1830s, electric telegraphy permitted "real time" communication at the speed of light—186,000 miles per second. Train station operators used telegraphs to route trains and prevent collisions. Weather scientists exploited the train network to gather weather information from frontier forts and towns. "I would frequently write upon the bulletin board . . . what and when weather changes were coming," one telegrapher wrote in 1846. "Frequently this was with such accuracy as to create considerable comment and wonder." In 1870, Congress charged the U.S. Army Signal Service with "taking meteorological observations at the military stations in the interior of the continent and at other points in the States and Territories . . . and for giving notice on the northern [Great] lakes and on the seacoast by magnetic telegraph and marine signals, of the approach and force of storms."

Early researchers such as James Pollard Espy realized that storms are caused by the ascent or convection of warm air. At higher altitudes the air expands and cools, so its water vapor condenses into water droplets visible in the form of clouds. Espy even suggested fighting droughts by setting enormous forest fires that would spawn rain clouds!

The second crucial discovery was that many storms *rotate*.

Nowadays every schoolchild knows that air spirals into a tornado. But most scientists didn't recognize this truth until the second half of the nineteenth century. Previously, they thought that tornadoes sucked up air in straight lines rather than in a spiralling fashion. In 1838, William C. Redfield investigated a New England tornado that resembled "the proboscis of an enormous elephant." He walked seven miles of the twister's path and analyzed the

TWISTER

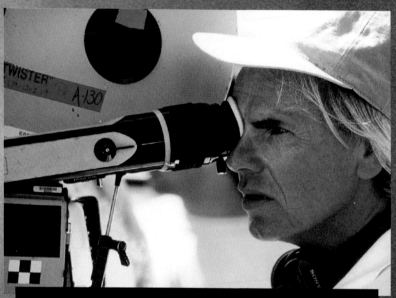

Director Jan De Bont composes his shot at the first tornado's irrigation ditch encounter. [DAVID JAMES]

Actors and camera crew are pummeled by the special effects crew's hail and debris for the "Hailstone Hill" sequence. [DAVID JAMES]

The small town of Wakita, Oklahoma, is "dressed" for the night sequence approaching Aunt Meg's house. [DAVID JAMES]

A 3,500-pound replica of a real tank truck being raised and prepped for the big explosion. [RON BATZDORFF]

Special effects crews use gasoline and primer cord to get the explosion of the tank truck at the F5 tornado. [RON BATZDORFF]

Jo and Bill Harding (Helen Hunt and Bill Paxton) watch as the F5 tornado grabs the dorothy and sucks up the sensors. [DAVID JAMES]

Jonas's team preps him for his tornadic encounter. Left to right: Patty (Melanie Hoops), Dean (Dean Lindsay), Tony (Anthony Rapp), Jake (Jake Busey). [DAVID JAMES]

In southwestern Oklahoma on the last week of VORTEX '95, Jerry Straka gazes at gathering storms from his and Josh Wurman's "Doppler on Wheels" mobile radar vehicle. [JIM REED]

A twister-toppled tractor-trailer lies on its side like a dead dinosaur in Corum, Oklahoma, on April 17, 1995. The driver was unhurt. [JIM REED]

A huge supercell thunderstorm near Laverne, Oklahoma, spawns a tornado just after sunset in May 1991. The twister passed through the Laverne outskirts and caused minor structural damage. [WARREN FAIDLEY]

A tornado passes through open country five miles south of Clearwater, Kansas, on May 16, 1991. [KEITH BREWSTER]

Multiple lightning bolts strike a southeastern Arizona city. [WARREN FAIDLEY]

directions in which trees fell. He concluded their orientation was "decisive evidence" of winds rotating around the tornado, "in the direction from right to left or which is contrary to the hands of a watch"—that is, counterclockwise or "cyclonically." Redfield's views led to a celebrated debate with Espy, who denied that tornadoes rotate at all.

Nowadays, we know that *almost* all tornadoes and *all* hurricanes in the Northern Hemisphere rotate cyclonically (but anticyclonically, that is, clockwise, in the Southern Hemisphere.) Why? The American scientist William Ferrel attributed their direction of rotation to the rotation of the Earth—specifically, to the Coriolis force.

The Coriolis effect is named for the nineteenth-century French physicist Gaspard-Gustave de Coriolis. As wind blows, Earth rotates beneath it. This causes the wind to appear to curve slightly. In the Northern Hemisphere the wind appears to curve to its right; in the Southern Hemisphere, to the left.

Ferrel was right about hurricanes—but *not* about tornadoes. Tornadoes are too small for their rotation to result directly from the Coriolis effect. (Another popular myth is that the Coriolis force makes toilets flush clockwise in the Northern Hemisphere and counterclockwise in the Southern Hemisphere!) However, almost all Northern Hemisphere tornadoes rotate counterclockwise anyway because they inherit the counterclockwise motion of their parent storms.

Ferrel correctly explained how a tornado develops

its low air pressure. It spins so rapidly that air accelerates outward, preventing air from rushing into the funnel from its sides. Instead, new air penetrates the funnel through its lower tip, as in a vacuum cleaner. This slows the ability of the funnel to replace air sucked up by the updraft, and drives the air pressure even lower. Air pressure inside tornado funnels probably drops by about 10 percent—equal to about a 2-inch drop of a barometer. Similar pressure drops also occur during hurricanes.

The discovery of tornadoes' rotation helped nineteenth-century physicists explain their extraordinary violence—in part, anyway. This partial explanation is based on the "law of the conservation of angular momentum." The best-known example of angular momentum is a spinning skater. Watch Nancy Kerrigan on TV as she spins with her arms outstretched. What happens as she wraps her arms around herself: She spins much faster, right? Why? A scientist would describe Nancy's energy in terms of momentum (her velocity multiplied by her mass). The angular momentum law says her velocity multiplied by the radius of her spin must equal a constant value. Therefore, if she changes her radius, then her rotational velocity must also change to keep the constant "constant."

Likewise, nineteenth-century scientists assumed that large, vertical columns of air such as cyclones start spinning and gradually contract. As they contract, they spin faster and faster until (thanks to the law of the conservation of angular momentum) they're spinning at hundreds of miles per hour. This didn't fully explain the tornado's violence, as we shall see. But it was a step in the right direction.

✦

Sergeant John Park Finley was America's first real tornado expert. In the 1870s, he inspected twister damage by touring the Western states by horse and buggy. He made meticulous maps of farms that showed the exact paths and impacts of tornadoes. (One Finley map included a curved line that represented the aerial path of a hired man, whom a tornado blew 400 feet.) He found that the worst damage was confined to narrow areas that averaged 1,400 feet wide, and that few twisters traveled more than 20 miles. He marveled at the "most terrific" damage near Irving, Kansas, where a new iron and steel bridge was "completely twisted into shapeless ruin."

Finley also pioneered tornado climatology, the study of tornado frequencies. He enlisted more than 2,400 volunteers for a tornado-observing network. They initially reported an average of 10 to 60 tornadoes per year. In 1880, the annual count passed 100 for the first time. (The present annual average exceeds 1,000!) "Without this man's perseverance, there would probably be no [nineteenth-century tornado] records of value," said tornado climatologist Thomas P. Grazulis.

Finley also began forecasting tornadoes. In 1879, he advised the War Department to post a weather observer in Kansas City during tornado season. The observer could telegraph news of severe storms to points east. "To get the right information to the proper point before the occurrence of the dangerous [tornado] phenomenon, thereby affording opportunity to provide against its ravages, is the great desideratum. It can be done." He began issuing his own forecasts in 1884, based on limited weather data from across the nation. Unfortunately, weather stations were few and far between, especially in the tornado-plagued Midwest.

After several years, Finley's bosses decided that tornado forecasting was a bad idea: It might spark panics. So the Signal Service banned the use of the word *tornado* in forecasts. The U.S. government didn't resume tornado forecasting until the mid-twentieth century. The rest of Finley's program soon withered and died.

The 1930s brought the Depression, war scares, and terrible weather to America. One of the decade's ghastliest tornado outbreaks struck the South on the evening of April 5, 1936. Elvis Presley was fifteen months old when an incredible tornado ripped through his hometown of Tupelo, Mississippi. His mother, Gladys, "clung to her baby and huddled in fear in their small house," says biographer Patricia Jobe Pierce. "The tornado leveled St. Mark's Methodist Church across from the Presleys' home and flattened other shacks along the street . . . years later Gladys convinced Elvis that God saved him that day (and the day he was born) because God had determined Elvis was 'born to be a great man.' "

Tragically, important scientific advances often stem from military research. During World War II, accurate weather forecasts were required to plan troop movements and to time bombing raids. For meteorologists, the war's biggest boon was radar. Radar, for radio detection and ranging, was meteorology's first major remote sensing tool.

Bomber pilots crossing the Atlantic made the war's top atmospheric discovery: the jet stream, a high-altitude, ever-meandering river of extremely strong winds (hundreds of miles per hour). The jet stream helps to energize and steer surface storms. Meteorologists increasingly used radiosonde balloons—battery-powered balloons with weather instruments and radio transmitters—to measure wind speeds and directions tens of thousands of feet above Earth. Understanding the current position and intensity of the jet stream and other high-altitude winds is vital for tornado forecasting.

During the war, the scientists Albert K. Showalter and Joe R. Fulks identified the weather factors that tend to precede thunderstorms. These include (in paraphrase):

   —A rapid temperature decrease with height. This encourages convection and, in turn, thundercloud formation.

—A distinct boundary between high surface humidity and a large, dry region high above. This spurs moist surface air to convect into the upper air, where it forms clouds.

—A temperature inversion, or warm layer of air over cooler surface air.

In the fight against twisters, radar scored its first big success in April 1956. At Texas A&M in College Station, Texas, researchers saw an approaching thunderstorm on a local radar unit. Analysts estimated that the storm would hit town about the same time that students left public schools. They contacted school officials and urged them to keep students in classes until the storm passed. The storm dropped a twister one block from a school. If students had been walking home as the funnel dropped, it could have slaughtered them.

We have come to realize that these vicious storms [tornadoes] are much more frequent and more widespread than used to be thought. They are most common in the Midwest, but tornadoes are now known to strike in every part of the country and at every season.
—Morris Tepper, *Scientific American* (1958)

Francis Reichelderfer was a visionary. Then in his late fifties, a former naval officer who oversaw the 17,000 employees of the Weather Bureau, he championed the early use of electronic computers for forecasting. Later he promoted the development of weather satellites. His main contribution to tornado science came in 1952, when he opened the Weather Bureau's Severe Local Storm Warning Center (SELS) in Washington, D.C.*

At 11:00 P.M. Eastern time on March 17, 1952, SELS issued its first tornado watch: "There is a possibility of tornadoes in eastern Texas and extreme southeastern Oklahoma tonight, spreading into southern Arkansas and Louisiana before daybreak."

The watch stayed in effect until 7:00 A.M. No one saw any tornadoes.

To improve tornado warnings, SELS acquired a "Tornado Research Airplane." In 1956 SELS contracted with a pilot, Jim Cook of Jacksboro, Texas, to fly his single-engine F-51 aircraft into stormy regions. He made his first tornado flights out of Dallas in April 1956. His plane carried instruments including thermometers, humidity gauges, air pressure instruments, wind gauges, and 35mm tracking cameras. He recorded his weather observations on a dictation machine.

*

SELS was the ancestor of today's National Severe Storms Forecast Center in Kansas City. NSSFC is the nation's first line of defense against tornadoes and other local severe storms. NSSFC meteorologists monitor the nation's weather 24 hours a day, 365 days a year, watching for large-scale changes—say, the birth of a mean-looking cold front, or an ominous shift in the jet stream—that could spawn thunderstorms, blizzards, floods, or other violent weather. (Hurricanes are handled by the National Hurricane Center in Miami.)

Cook's flights saved lives. For example, on a 1961 flight in a war surplus P-38, he spotted a funnel cloud over Oklahoma. It dangled (in the *Post*'s words) "like a dirty, oily rope." The funnel raced toward a town, "one of those quiet prairie places with a main street, a river, a railroad track, and a grain elevator. He was low enough to see children playing and people walking about. Obviously no one down there knew of the tornado. . . ." Cook radioed the Tulsa airport, hoping officials there could warn the town. Unfortunately, he didn't know the town's name. He struggled to explain to an air traffic controller that "it's near Henryetta and it lies near two little lakes." But electrical static drowned out his transmissions.

Time was running out, so he elected to warn the town himself. He lowered his P-38 and flew it directly down the town's main street at 200 miles per hour. The racket startled locals, who looked up and pointed. Then he veered the P-38 toward the tornado. As townspeople viewed his ascent, they noticed the funnel. He watched with relief as they rushed to backyard cellars and slammed the doors shut.

For the first time since Sergeant John Finley's brief, failed effort, the U.S. government was at war against tornadoes. Humans, the pursued, were now the pursuers, who chased tornadoes to dissect their secrets. But a handful of visionaries wanted to move beyond dissection, to the next logical step: extermination.

CHAPTER 4

"To Destroy Tornadoes Before They Destroy Us"

Baby boomers grew up watching television reruns of the 1939 movie *The Wizard of Oz*. No matter how many times this writer saw the film, he gasped every time he saw Dorothy and Toto's home sucked into the tornado funnel. It was an impressive special effect by the standards of the 1930s, and it is still convincing today.

In real life, many people have ventured into tornadoes. The best-known tale is told by Will Keller, a Kansas farmer. On June 22, 1928, a tornado hit his home. He smelled a "strong gassy odor," then

I looked up, and to my astonishment I saw right into the heart of the tornado. There was a circular opening in the center of the funnel, about fifty to one hundred feet in diameter and extending straight upward for a distance of at least half a mile, as best I could judge under the circumstances. The walls of this opening were rotating clouds and the whole was brilliantly lighted with constant flashes of lightning which zigzagged from side to side.

Keller's tale intrigued Bernard Vonnegut, who had co-pioneered cloud seeding with Vincent Schaefer and Irving Langmuir. An expert on atmospheric electricity, Vonnegut was especially interested in Keller's description of what might be unusual electrical events within the tornadoes—the "constant flashes of lightning." Vonnegut himself had witnessed the thunderstorm that spawned the murderous Worcester, Massachusetts, tornado of 1953. They generated "the most spectacular lightning I had ever seen . . . at least 20 lightning flashes per second." He calculated that the storm had generated about 100 million kilowatts of electricity, "roughly equivalent to the generating capacity of the entire United States." Could lightning be the covert fuel source for tornadoes?

It was an old idea. The science of atmospheric electricity was born in 1752, when Benjamin Franklin flew history's most famous kite into a thunderstorm. The kite hung from a silk thread, at the end of which dangled a metal key. During the storm, Franklin reached for the key. An electric spark leaped between the key and his hand. That spark proved that lightning is ordinary electricity. Anyone can generate electricity by walking across a rug, then reaching for a doorknob: A electric spark leaps between your hand and the knob.

Afterward, the electrical theory of tornadoes was largely forgotten—until it was rediscovered in the 1950s by Bernard Vonnegut. Through his long and sometimes controversial career, Vonnegut has pursued many offbeat ideas. Some are so offbeat that they'd seem at home in a novel by his younger brother, the satirist and science-fiction writer Kurt Vonnegut Jr. For example, Bernard was fascinated by farmers' reports that tornadoes defeathered their chickens. Could one estimate a tornado's wind speed by how thoroughly it defeathered a chicken? To find out, he placed chickens in a wind tunnel and turned on the fan. The fan blew off the feathers, but in an inconsistent manner. He concluded that defeathering was no substitute for a sturdy anemometer. He published his findings in a short scientific paper, entitled "Chicken Plucking as a Measure of Tornado Wind Speed."

He has long doubted the traditional theory of how tornadoes form (tornadogenesis). In 1960, Vonnegut suggested they were on the wrong track. In "Electrical Theory of Tornadoes," an article for the *Journal of Geophysical Research,* he calculated that the tornado updraft is much too strong to be blamed on ordinary temperature differences in the air. Something else must be driving the updraft. That something could be lightning or other manifestations of atmospheric electricity. Perhaps lightning bolts repeatedly flashed in the same place, heating it and creating intense convection—that is, an updraft—in a narrow column. Start the column rotating, and you have a tornado. (Alternately, he said, the storm's electric field might accelerate electrically charged atoms to high speed.)

Where was all this leading? In his 1960 paper, Vonnegut offered a prophecy:

> If tornadoes are caused by electrical mechanisms, then through better understanding of these mechanisms it should be possible to increase the accuracy of tornado forecasts, to obtain warning of their presence, and, conceivably, to inhibit or prevent their formation.

By coincidence, other scientists were *already* trying to suppress lightning—not because they wanted to stop tornadoes, but because lightning itself is a major natural hazard. A lightning-suppression program called Project Skyfire had been operated since the early 1950s by several federal agencies, including the Weather Bureau, the Departments of Interior and Agriculture, the National Science Foundation, and the President's Advisory Committee on Weather Control. They hoped to prevent lightning from starting forest fires and hitting sensitive facilities such as airports, missile bases, and nuclear weapons storage sites.

Lightning occurs when different parts of a thundercloud develop opposite electrical charges (negative and positive). Then a huge spark (a lightning bolt) leaps between the negative and positive areas, neutralizing them. Scientists reasoned that if they could *slowly* neutralize the cloud, then the charge differences might remain too slight to trigger lightning.

The September 22, 1967, issue of *Science* ran a paper titled, "Tornadoes: Mechanism and Control." Its author was a forty-two-year-old physicist, Stirling A. Colgate, a veteran of the U.S. hydrogen bomb and nuclear fusion energy programs. Colgate's paper began: "The possibility that the energy source of tornadoes is primarily electrical has been suggested independently by several authors, the most convincing analysis being given by Vonnegut." He claimed that ordinary atmospheric theories "cannot adequately account" for tornado wind speeds, which he believed were "close to Mach 1" (the speed of sound).

Could one snuff out tornadoes as one turns off a lightbulb—by switching off their sources of electricity? Colgate said that, to date, lightning suppression experiments with wires "have met with only partial success . . . presumably because the cloud itself is an insulating medium and will support large internal [electrical] fields without breaking down to the wires."

He suggested an alternate method: Inject tons of a negatively charged gas and "a fine aerosol of smoke particles" into the thundercloud. These might deelectrify the cloud before it could spawn tornadoes. For tornado suppression, ten tons of the gas might do the job. True, ten tons "is a large mass to inject rapidly adjacent to or inside the tornado, but is perhaps feasible from an airplane. Much larger quantities of borate are dropped on forest fires."

At about the same time, Vernon Rossow was working at NASA's Ames Research Center, just south of San Francisco. He was a bright forty-year-old expert on fluid dynamics and had just won NASA's Super Performance Award. In 1966, *Time* magazine wrote about his lab experiments to demonstrate links between electricity and tornadoes. He wanted to fire long wires into clouds to suppress lightning, thereby "robbing the tornado of the energy needed to sustain it," the magazine said.

By 1967, Rossow decided to conduct initial experiments on waterspouts. Waterspouts are weaker than tornadoes and, therefore, safer to work around. They are also more frequent than tornadoes, and therefore easier to locate. He headed for the waterspout-haunted Florida Keys, where he hoped "to fire wire-deploying projectiles into the cloud over any waterspout within range."

The age of tornado control was finally dawning. Or so it appeared. Even the world's most respected tornado expert took the topic seriously. To the news media, T. Theodore Fujita of the University of Chicago was "Mr. Tornado." In 1972 *National Geographic* ran a full-page color photo of Fujita playing with a miniature tornado—a swirling column of vapor—in his laboratory. Said Fujita: "I hope that within ten years we will learn from experiments like these how to modify real tornadoes."

The Florida Keys is a string of islands sprinkled through gorgeous blue-green waters south of the Sunshine State. For five weeks, Rossow and his NASA colleague Harold Clements patrolled the warm seas, searching the horizon for waterspouts. They didn't want to fire until they were within range of a waterspout cloud. Sixteen times they saw waterspouts from the boats—white threads dangling from cumulus clouds. But they never came close enough to fire. Waterspouts are will-o'-the-wisps, like mirages; chase one, and it may disappear before you reach it.

Eventually they abandoned the waterspout-modification experiment. On September 30, 1968, after flying near 52 waterspouts, Rossow concluded in his report to NASA that "electricity does not play a primary role in [waterspouts'] structure and could be eliminated as a generating mechanism or as a means of identification."

Indeed, atmospheric electricity seemed more likely to *destroy* waterspouts than to create them. On August 9, 1967, while gazing through binoculars, Rossow saw a lightning bolt near a waterspout funnel. The bolt "caused the funnel to break into pieces as if made of glass. . . . The pieces drifted apart slightly as they evaporated" and disappeared in a minute.

In his report, Rossow cautioned that he had been observing waterspouts, not tornadoes. Perhaps electricity triggered tornadoes but not waterspouts. Even so, his experiment marked the beginning of the decline of Vonnegut's electrical theory of tornadogenesis. In 1975, Robert Davies-Jones and Joseph H. Golden of NSSL wrote in the *Journal of Geophysical Research* that during their chases, they found no evidence to support Vonnegut's theory. Chasers rarely saw lightning near tornadoes. They also surveyed tornado tracks, checking for evidence of unusual electrical activity—say, scorched ground. They found none.

Also by that time, they noted, one of Vonnegut's central assumptions—that tornadic winds approach the speed of sound—had collapsed. Scientists had analyzed motion-picture films of tornadoes to estimate how fast they were rotating. They also surveyed building damage to estimate what wind speeds would create such wreckage. Their conclusion: Twister winds never exceeded 300 mph, and most were less than 200 mph.

Tornado experts frequently cite the Davies-Jones-Golden paper as the one that nixed the debate over electricity and tornadoes.

Vonnegut hasn't given up. In 1990 the elderly, amiable scientist flew to Plainfield, Illinois, to interview and videotape eyewitnesses who reported seeing eerie electrical effects during a tornado.

However, almost all tornado experts agree that Vonnegut's theory is a dead duck. By the mid-1990s, hundreds of storm chasers had videotaped tornadoes at close range; the tapes show little, if any, unusual lightning activity close to funnels. If there's any link between tornadoes and atmospheric electricity, then the link must be very subtle indeed.

*T*he demise of the electrical theory didn't kill hopes for tornado control. In fact, the topic was discussed vigorously in the late 1960s and early 1970s.

Gordon J. F. MacDonald of UCLA, a member of President Johnson's Science Advisory Committee, thought cloud seeding or other means to trigger small changes in weather would cascade into larger effects that might, with any luck, weaken or suffocate a tornado.

One strategy required the generation of "hot spots"—areas of artificial convection—that might destabilize or block tornadoes. Scientists could generate a hot spot by affixing jet engines to the ground and pointing them upward. They would exhaust "half a ton of air per second at a speed of 1,000 ft./sec.," thereby creating a hot updraft. The updraft could spawn local clouds and perhaps precipitation, which might suck energy from another storm that threatened to turn tornadic. (Alternately, the rain might create a cold downdraft that might weaken the tornado.) However, the plan could backfire: The jet engines might themselves spawn a severe storm!

Scientists might also form a hot spot by burning large containers of oil or coal. The French researcher Henri Dessens had already built such a facility—called Meteotron—in France. He burned enormous amounts of fuel in hopes (never realized) of generating significant amounts of rainfall. (Ironically, the blaze created small tornadoes!)

Another possibility, NSSL director Edwin Kessler said, was to "alter the Earth's topography and roughness so as to decrease the probability of tornadoes over inhabited areas—perhaps by building special-purpose mounds or ridges or by planting wind-resisting vegetation." Scientists had long debated whether terrain affects tornadoes. Long ago, they thought that minor topographical features (such as hills) could divert twisters. They no longer believe this (nor do the residents of Barneveld, Wisconsin, and Topeka, Kansas). But laboratory experiments and field observations hint that "rough" terrains such as forests or buildings in large cities may weaken tornadoes. If so, then one might protect a city by, say, planting a forest around it.

Others advocated a more aggressive approach. In the late 1960s and 1970s, a few researchers used laboratory models of tornadoes to investigate ways to destroy real-life twisters with explosives. An aerospace engineer, T. Maxworthy of the University of Southern California, suggested testing the scheme by detonating explosives inside small desert vortices called dust devils.

Would-be tornado controllers weren't merely daydreaming. They were motivated by a fear of future disasters on an unparalleled scale. That fear was worsened by the events of April 3 and 4, 1974, when the nation experienced its worst recorded tornado outbreak. An incredible 30 tornadoes ranking F4 or F5, plus many more of weaker size (the total number of tornadoes may have approached 150) raked the Eastern United States. Their roughly parallel paths ran across a map like scratches from a gigantic cat's claw. More than 300 people died, 34 of them in a single town—Xenia, Ohio.

The 1974 cataclysm especially troubled officials in a then-thriving U.S. business: the nuclear power industry.

What would happen if a twister hit a nuclear plant? Were the plants sturdy enough to withstand the tornado's fierce winds? And if not, would the tornado spew poisonous, scalding-hot radioactivity over the countryside? Could a tornado unleash a nuclear catastrophe, rendering much of a state uninhabitable? To find answers, the U.S. Atomic Energy Commission and its successor, the Nuclear Regulatory Commission or NRC, funded extensive research on tornadoes from the 1960s into the 1980s. Specifically, the NRC needed to know: Are tornadoes violent enough and frequent enough to threaten commercial nuclear reactors? And if so, how can nuclear engineers redesign reactors to make them twister-proof? The key questions were:

(1) How fast are a tornado's fastest winds?

(2) What is the internal "structure" of a tornado?

(3) How frequent are severe tornadoes?

The NRC needed answers to these and other questions fairly quickly. By the 1970s, nuclear power was controversial; its base of political support was fragile. A single devastating accident could wreck the industry.

On April 18, 1978, Robert F. Abbey Jr. of the NRC called Ted Fujita, also known as Mr. Tornado. Abbey asked Fujita to fly to Mississippi and do something that Fujita had done many times before—survey a tornado's damage path. But the Mississippi tornado was unique: It had just hit a nuclear power plant.

Fortunately, the plant's reactor hadn't been operational at the time. The facility was still under construction. But what if it had been operational? Would the plant have withstood the blow? Or would the reactor containment vessel have ruptured? Fujita hoped to find out.

On reaching Mississippi, Fujita flew in a small airplane over the tornado's path. He snapped numerous photos as the Cessna 182 soared over the 18-mile trail of debris and destruction, which climaxed at the half-completed Grand Gulf nuclear power plant near Port Gibson.

During Fujita's flight he passed over Lake Brun, an oxbow lake—so called because of its crescent shape. Near Lake Brun was a flattened forest. Fujita studied the orientation of the fallen trees. Until recent years, he would have assumed that the tornado had knocked the trees down. But if that were the case, then all the trees should have fallen in the same direction while the twister, moving horizontally over the ground, mowed them down. Instead, the trees spread out radially (in all directions), as if hit by an immense force from *above*.

To Fujita, the radially toppled trees were an increasingly familiar sight. He had seen similar damage on numerous flights. By the late 1970s, he claimed he had discovered the cause: a "downburst" or "microburst," a surge of cold air that plunged from a thunderstorm. (Likewise, an egg dropped vertically to the floor splatters out in all directions.) Fujita claimed that some "tornado" damage was actually caused by downbursts. Originally controversial, his downburst theory is now generally accepted.

Fujita first surveyed a tornado track from an airplane in 1965. Over the next twenty-six years, he and his associates flew over more than 300 tracks and snapped some 30,000 photos. During his early flights, he noticed strange patterns in the cornfields. The patterns resembled a repeating sequence of letter *C*'s that slightly overlapped.

A decade earlier, the researcher E. L. Van Tassel had noticed similar cycloidal marks in tornado tracks. Van Tassel proposed the marks were huge scratches, gouged out of the ground by debris swirling in the tornado. He calculated the debris could gouge out the marks if the winds were blowing close to 500 mph.

In 1967 Fujita visited a tornado trail in Illinois on the ground and got a close-up look at cycloidal marks. Sure enough, they weren't scratches; they were debris. How could a tornado—a simple vortex—arrange debris into such neat geometric patterns?

The answer: A tornado *isn't* always a simple, spiraling vortex! Rather, it may include a number of smaller vortices, which orbit the larger, central vortex like satellites orbiting the Earth. Fujita suspected the tornado's strongest winds were concentrated at the small vortices, which he called "suction vortices."

The discovery of suction vortices had important implications for the NRC research. The bad news was that suction vortices were extraordinarily violent, by far the windiest part of the funnel, but they were restricted to small parts of the tornado. Their small size and complex motion made it hard to figure out how wind stresses would be distributed around a nuclear plant. But that was also the good news: Only small parts of the tornado contained the worst winds, not the entire funnel. That lessened the chance that the highest winds would strike a sensitive structure. Based on his new interpretation of the cycloidal marks, Fujita concluded that Van Tassel had seriously overestimated the tornadic wind speeds; they were substantially lower than 500 mph. That, too, was good news for nuclear plant designers.

Tornado pranks are legendary. Countless American legends tell of twisters that ripped apart a well-built home but ignored a nearby shack, or that leveled the home but left a goldfish bowl standing in the living room. How can such events happen? Because the suction vortices are extremely selective: They concentrate the highest winds in extremely small areas.

Fujita made one of his most remarkable and grisly observations at Lubbock, Texas, in 1970, after two tornadoes smashed the town. He showed that the vast majority of deaths occurred precisely where the suction vortices touched down—that is, along the cycloidal pathways. The random destruction of tornadoes is a myth; their choreography obeys a lethal geometry.

Lubbock was a city of 170,000 with a passion for football and little experience with twisters. The last tornado had struck the town in 1900. The inhabitants—like the residents of many moderate-size urban areas—assumed "it won't happen here." At 8:10 P.M. on the evening of May 11, 1970, the first, weaker twister arrived. It passed over an unfinished highway interchange and blew 13 beams off the overpass. Each beam weighed more than 50 tons. At 9:45 a fiercer tornado buzz-sawed from downtown Lubbock to the airport.

When Fujita arrived in town, he observed that the

first tornado had knocked down only 13 of the 35 available beams. Why did it leave the other 22 standing? Simple: because the cycloidal paths of the suction vortices took them over the 13 beams. They missed the other 22. To prove his case, he mapped the cycloidal debris paths with his usual meticulousness.

The twisters hurled a freight car more than 200 feet from its track, and blew a 16-ton empty fertilizer tank a half mile. Fujita concluded the huge tank had been airborne for two-thirds of its trip (at one point it passed over a four-lane federal highway). A "small wooden shack in a direct path of the second tornado was found to be practically undamaged because it was standing between suction [vortices]."

Later Fujita flew in a helicopter over the second tornado path. He observed debris marking the cycloidal paths of the suction vortices. He mapped the cycloidal trails. Then he marked the site of every fatality on the same map. To his amazement, *95 percent* of all fatalities occurred where the suction vortices had struck.

The Fujita Scale is based substantially on Fujita's Lubbock research. The scale was a big step toward a long-sought tool: a way to classify tornado strengths quantitatively, just as astronomers classify stars according to their specific masses, colors, and other traits. Tornado investigators use the Fujita Scale to estimate the severity of a tornado based on how much damage it causes. Tornadoes that are ranked F0 are called gale tornadoes: They break off tree branches and topple trees with shallow roots. An F1 or "moderate" tornado may overturn a mobile home and damage roofs. An F2 ("significant") tornado can uproot a big tree and wreck a mobile home. An F3 ("severe") tornado may tip over a train and throw a car off the road. An F4 ("devastating") tornado can destroy a well-built home and toss cars through the air. An F5 ("incredible," such as the Barneveld tornado) twister can damage steel-reinforced concrete buildings and hurl missiles as big as cars for hundreds of feet.

In the 1970s, NSSFC director Allen Pearson modified the scale by adding specifics on the path length and width of each tornado type. The modified scale's categories are:

THE FUJITA-PEARSON SCALE

Scale	Wind Speed	Path Length	Path Width
0	40–72 mph	0.3–0.9 miles	6–17 yards
1	73–112 mph	1.0–3.1 miles	18–55 yards
2	113–157 mph	3.2–9.9 miles	56–175 yards
3	158–206 mph	10–31 miles	176–566 yards
4	207–260 mph	32–99 miles	0.3–0.9 miles
5	261–318 mph	100–315 miles	1.0–3.1 miles

Initially, some meteorologists didn't accept Fujita's theory of suction vortices. The idea gradually won acceptance for several reasons: First, researchers simulated suction vortices in miniature "tornadoes" in the laboratory. Second, they observed suction vortex-like objects in dust devils, which are smaller versions of tornadoes. And third, they found eyewitness and photographic evidence of suction vortices in past tornadoes—some of them more than a century ago!

The so-called tornado machine is one of the most useful and entertaining tools in tornado science. These laboratory devices use whirling fans and smoke generators to create small whirlwinds, typically several feet high. The whirlwinds are often amazingly similar to real-life tornadoes and waterspouts. Scientists analyze how air moves through the mini-twisters by spraying particles into them— say, confetti, sawdust, or soap bubbles. They measure air pressure inside the funnels by sliding small instruments into the vortices, or by scanning them with a laser beam.

Scientists use tornado machines to explore questions such as: Why do tornadoes come in so many shapes and sizes? Why are some tornadoes smooth, finger-like funnels while others are boiling, turbulent maelstroms? What causes suction vortices? Is a tornado one big updraft, or does it have a narrow downdraft in its core? How is a tornado affected by the terrain it passes over? How reliable are computer simulations of tornadoes? A few have used the machines to probe the boldest question of all: Is there any way to modify or "kill" a tornado?

One of the biggest tornado machines is at Purdue University in West Lafayette, Indiana. John T. Snow built and operated this device in the 1970s and

1980s. The machine is a cylinder, 9 feet tall and 9 feet wide. At the top is a fan, which pumps air from the cylinder. At the bottom, a rotating screen stirs air into rotation. Vents emit swirling white vapor into the cylinder. As air ascends in the rotating updraft, a vortex quickly forms.

In the early 1970s, the tornado researcher Neil Ward simulated suction vortices in a tornado machine. He inserted air pressure–measuring devices into the mini-suction vortices. Their air pressures were "much lower" than in the primary vortex. Ward's work convinced many scientists that Fujita's suction vortices were real.

Do tornadoes have "eyes"? Everyone has heard about the hurricane's "eye"—a calm area at the center of the cyclone. Inside the eye, winds may drop to zero and clouds may disappear. The sun or stars may come out. Ironically, the passage of a hurricane eye is dangerous because unwary people leave shelter, thinking the storm has passed. Within minutes the other side of the storm strikes. Those who left the shelter may die.

Likewise, a few people briefly trapped inside tornadoes observed that the interior winds were calm. In 1962, a tornado passed through Newton, Kansas; witnesses said the center of the vortex was quiet, but smaller funnels "were appearing all around town at different locations, moving in various directions." (Were those "funnels" suction vortices?) The veteran chaser Howard Bluestein has seen a few wall clouds with eyelike features. In one case in 1978, he drove under a wall cloud in Oklahoma "and noted a bright, hollow, cylindrical tube extending upward." (Is that the true explanation for Roy Hall's "brilliant cloud"?)

Hurricanes develop eyes because warm air high above the storm sinks downward. As it sinks, it evaporates clouds, creating the eye, a "hole" in the storm that is obvious on satellite photos. For many years, scientists suspected that something similar happens in tornadoes. Ward and other scientists used tornado machines to create micro-twisters, then tossed confetti and other particles into them to see how air flowed through them. Sure enough, they observed a slender column of sinking air within the vortices. Later, VORTEX radar scientists scanned tornadoes and concluded that air was sinking in their interior.

That sinking air may also explain suction vortices. As the air sinks, it encounters rising air. The result is similar to what happens when a crowd of people ascending a staircase meets a crowd in descent: turbulence, as everyone scrambles to get around everyone else. In tornadoes that turbulence is called vortex breakdown. Vortex breakdown allows the lower part of the tornado to disintegrate into several smaller, independent whirlwinds—the suction vortices.

And that leads us to a fascinating question: Are big cities immune to tornadoes?

A strange fact haunts the history of tornadoes: Certain major cities have experienced remarkably few twisters. Consider Chicago: Tornadoes have raged throughout the Chicago suburbs over the last century, but almost never penetrated the densely populated downtown. Why? Is it just a coincidence—a lucky break for the Windy City? Or is there something about Chicago and other large cities that *repels* tornadoes?

In the early 1970s, Fujita conducted an interesting experiment. Using his tornado machine, he simulated a tornado's attack on downtown Chicago. He placed small rocks at the base of the machine to simulate skyscrapers and a small pool of water to represent Lake Michigan. He placed heating wires under the rocks to mimic the city's heat. (Cities tend to be warmer than their surroundings because of machinery, pollution, human bodies, and reflectivity from artificial surfaces such as glass buildings.) When he switched on the "tornado," the misty funnel thrived until it hit the rocks. Then it weakened. It started to break up when he boosted the heat. Afterward, he speculated that tornadoes thrive on a steady diet of warm air. Perhaps big cities' rising warm air is too unstable to feed strong tornadoes.

Fujita also analyzed the history of tornadoes in Chicago and Tokyo. He found a horseshoe-shaped area of downtown Chicago that "appears to be tornado free during the past 20 years." He found the same effect in Tokyo, where the "tornado frequency appears to decrease toward the center of the city and toward the outer suburbs as well." He noted that Chicago's and Tokyo's populations were, respectively, 7 and 11 million people. Sticking his neck way out scientifically, he suggested that a city might possess a "threshold population" of 4 million for "effective tornado suppression."

Likewise, in 1977 C. R. Snider studied 244 Michigan tornadoes and concluded that large cities have disproportionately fewer tornadoes than small towns. The likelihood of a tornado is "approximately *inversely* proportional to the size of the city," he declared. "Large cities seem to resist tornado touchdowns."

A few years after his initial Chicago experiment, Fujita seemed to back away from its most extreme implications. "Despite such experimental evidence, we are not certain if the heat generated in Chicago is sufficient to kill all tornadoes. Existence of the tornado-free area in Chicago might be just accidental. Until more research is done, we should not simply assume a false sense of tornado security in our city. A large, violent tornado might manage to smash through the Loop, damaging skyscrapers and causing showers of window glass onto the streets."

However controversial some of his conclusions, Fujita's research revolutionized scientists' understanding of the inner world of tornadoes. Twisters, as it turned out, had an elegant inner geometry that varied from moment to moment during their lives.

That geometry caused their wind speeds to vary from place to place within the funnel. And that fact, in turn, greatly complicated the task of determining their likely impact on buildings, from ordinary homes to nuclear power plants.

But a crucial question lingered: How did tornadoes acquire their vicious energy? To answer that question, it wasn't enough to study films of tornadoes, or to survey their debris paths after they had passed. Rather, it was necessary to penetrate the tornado funnel itself—to pierce it with an instrumented probe that would radio back information about the interior. That task—the scientific world's version of Dorothy and Toto's flight on the whirlwind—would prove much more difficult and dangerous than expected.

CHAPTER 5

Into the Whirlwind

Humans have always ventured into forbidden places. They've spelunked in deep caves, ridden submarines to the ocean's darkest depths, and defied superstitious edicts by penetrating the crypt of Tutankhamen. Likewise, people have dreamed of venturing into a tornado. Many have, usually unwittingly. Only a few have lived to talk about it.

✦

In 1899, a twister hit Kirksville, Missouri, and blew two women and a boy over a church. They landed more than a thousand feet away, unharmed. "I was conscious all the time I was flying through the air . . ." one woman later said. "I seemed to be lifted up and whirled round and round, going up to a great height, at one time far above the church steeples. . . . As I was going through the air, being whirled about at the sport of the storm, I saw a horse soaring and rotating about with me. It was a white horse and had a harness on. By the way it kicked and struggled as it was hurled about I knew it was live. I prayed God that the horse might not come in contact with me, and it did not."

In 1959, by accident, Marine Lieutenant Colonel William H. Rankin got a close-up view of a thunderstorm's inner hell. On July 26, he took off in an F8U Crusader jet fighter from a North Carolina military base, bound for Massachusetts. He wasn't wearing a pressure suit—only "ordinary pilots' coveralls." Seeing thunderstorms in Virginia, he tried to fly over them. Then his engine's red warning light flickered. Fearing an explosion, he ejected nine miles above the Earth. The outside air was painfully cold—70 degrees below zero. Blue sheets of lightning exploded around him. His chute automatically opened. Then began his roller-coaster ride through the storm, as updrafts and downdrafts repeatedly flung him up and down. Intense rain almost drowned him, "as though I were at the bottom of a swimming pool." He repeatedly vomited. Baseball-size hail battered him senseless. At one point he stared "down into a long, black tunnel, a nightmarish corridor in space." (A mesocyclone? An embryonic tornado funnel?) "Sometimes, not wanting to see what was going on, I shut my eyes."

After forty minutes he landed ignominiously: He crashed into a tree trunk. A passing motorist gave him a ride. After a hospital stay—which included a brief bout of mild amnesia—he returned to active duty. He later described his adventure in an article for the *Saturday Evening Post* and a book, *The Man Who Rode the Thunder*.

Even more incredibly, in 1963 an entire commercial DC-8 jetliner may have flown through a tornado funnel! On the late morning of November 9, 1963, Eastern Air Lines flight 301 left New York City, bound for Mexico City. It carried 128 passengers. The pilots were Captain N. H. French and First Officer Grant Newby. The plane encountered thunderstorms over the Gulf of Mexico and stopped in Houston for refueling. Then it took off again. French planned to lift the plane to a cruising altitude of 31,000 feet. At 18,000 feet the plane passed through a cloud layer. French later testified at a Civil Aeronautics Board (CAB) hearing that just before entering the clouds,

I could see visually this heavy dark area to my left. On the right I could see visually a small dark area. In other words, it looked like a [thunderstorm] cell over on the right. However, my airplane radar did not show any echo for the cell on the right-hand side, or to the north. The radar did show the heavy band of dark area on the south and to my left. So on this 270-degree heading, we continued to climb and continued on up. There was a third cloud formation and the cloud formation was in the form of a sort of arch, that appeared to be an arch between a cell on the right and a cell on the left.

At 19,300 feet, something went terribly awry. French, Newby, and the flight engineer were watching two different air speed monitors. The monitors indicated their speed had dropped to *zero*. They stared at the dials for a moment, dumbfounded. Suddenly, the floor fell out from under them and the plane went into a steep dive. They couldn't believe their eyes.

Back in the passenger cabin, numerous passengers hurtled from their chairs. "I was just glued to the ceiling," Robert L. Monahan of Ocean City, New Jersey, later said.

Faster and faster the DC-8 plunged, its speed accelerating to an astonishing nine-tenths of the speed of sound. Newby wrestled frantically with the flight gear, struggling to save his stricken plane. He pushed the engines into idle reverse thrust. This maneuver (which tornado analyst Ferdinand C. Bates later called "one of the most amazing maneuvers of modern aviation") may have rescued the airplane. The DC-8 slowed down and gradually lifted.

Twelve seconds later, Newby heard a loud SNAP! The plane's number three jet engine had broken off and hurtled to Earth.

It took the crew two minutes to regain full control

of the plane, using their three surviving jet engines. They had fallen 14,000 feet—almost 3 miles—before recovering. The Civil Aeronautics Board launched an investigation of the near-tragedy.

During the hearing, French made an incredible claim: His DC-8 had flown into a tornado. He insisted there was no other explanation for his plane's extraordinary behavior.

Several years later, Bates, a researcher at St. Louis University, concluded that French was right: He had flown into a tornado funnel. Puzzling aspects of the flight made sense, Bates said, if one made an unusual assumption: The tornado was inclined to the horizontal. He stressed that the DC-8's air speed had plunged to zero. *"There is no maneuver in which the indicated air speed of a DC-8 can be brought to zero in flight in a no-wind environment. . . . The* only *way such an air-speed decrease can take place is through the penetration of a gradient of tail-to-nose wind so intense that the aircraft cannot initially respond. . . . The only phenomenon we know which contains such a wind speed and gradient,"* Bates said, "is the tornado." [His emphasis.]

Bates urged scientists to learn more about the tornado threat to aviation, perhaps by "dropping or launching . . . tracers and probes" into funnels. Others had similar ideas. Soon they would turn their ideas into action—not on tornadoes but, rather, on their watery counterpart, the waterspout.

In the late 1960s, a young doctoral student from Florida State, Joseph Golden, was flying with a friend over the Florida Keys. It was strictly a pleasure flight. But Golden's life changed when, gazing out over the blue-green waters, he spotted a waterspout. "We were screaming and yelling, as excited as kids at a football game. I had a brand-new movie camera with me, a Super 8, and it was the first time I had ever used it." He filmed the waterspout from a mile or two away.

The sight changed his career. He and several colleagues would spend years studying the waterspouts in unprecedented detail.

On Golden's early research flights, he rented a plane and told the pilot to fly near waterspouts. As he passed the funnels, Golden threw smoke flares from the plane. The smoke trails revealed the direction of air currents around the waterspouts. The waterspouts appeared to form along boundaries between different currents of air—say, between warm sea air and cold outflow from rainy cumulus clouds. He also tossed out balloons and confetti.

Golden and other scientists wanted to gather information from *within* the waterspout funnels. How low did air pressure fall within the funnel? Did the vortex column contain a core of sinking air?

Golden discussed the possibility of flying through waterspouts with Peter Sinclair, a scientist who had chased Arizona dust devils with an instrumented jeep. They prepared to fly through the waterspouts in a sturdy two-seater aircraft, an AT-6 trainer plane of World War II vintage. They covered the plane with weather instruments to measure conditions within the funnel.

The day arrived. The AT-6 taxied and took off. They prowled the skies until they spotted a waterspout. From a distance, it resembled a thread; closer in, a smooth veil. It hung from the asphalt-black underbelly of a cumulus congestus cloud. They flew under the cloud toward the funnel. In the growing darkness, Golden sat behind the pilot with "white knuckles and gritted teeth, holding on for dear life." A fraction of a second before they penetrated the funnel, Golden saw that its surface wasn't smooth; it was a turbulent swirl of vapor. Then he felt a jolt, his head struck the canopy, and they were inside the vortex. Less than one second later they flew out the other side.

Stirling Colgate traces his fascination with tornadoes to a lifelong love of explosions. He explains that he grew up in the countryside, where "you're always involved with dynamite. On farms back in the 1930s, you didn't have tractors to uproot stumps. You had dynamite." He has spent most of his career studying different types of explosions—from nuclear weapons blasts to exploding stars to accidental explosions at nuclear power plants. "And the tornado is a kind of atmospheric explosion."

Despite his rural upbringing, he was the child of privilege—the heir to a famous name and a huge family fortune based on toothpaste. Science fascinated him as a boy. "I was called a 'professor' at home when I was four or five years old. I suppose I made my first electric motor when I was eight." He attended the prestigious Los Alamos Ranch School in the mountains of New Mexico. In the early 1940s, as America entered the Second World War, two mysterious men arrived at Los Alamos. One wore a porkpie hat and called himself Mr. Smith; the other sported a fedora and identified himself as Mr. Jones. Shortly after their arrival, the erudite young Colgate glanced through a textbook, saw their pictures, and realized their real names: J. Robert Oppenheimer and Ernest O. Lawrence. "At that moment, I knew what they were working on, even though it was secret. They were planning to build an atomic bomb."

Los Alamos was converted from a boys' school to the nation's first atomic weapons laboratory. After growing up and receiving his doctoral degree at Cornell, Colgate worked at three federal labs—including Los Alamos—on nuclear bombs and other subjects.

Colgate didn't just work on "nukes," however. The nation's nuclear weapons labs were open to people with wide, even eccentric, interests. Through his career, Colgate has ventured into subjects far from his core interests or expertise—volcanoes, AIDS epidemiology, nuclear power, cosmology, tornadoes.

Colgate became interested in weather in the mid-1960s, when he became president of New Mexico Institute of Mining and Technology in Socorro, New Mexico. He got to know scientists at the school including E. J. Workman, a thunderstorm expert working on lightning suppression, and Vonnegut's close colleague Moore. As a private pilot, Colgate helped Vonnegut and Moore to erect one of their grandiose experiments to alter the electrical charge on clouds. The experiment involved stretching long, elevated wires between two mountain peaks. Flying his own aircraft, Colgate draped the wire between the peaks.

In 1985, at age fifty, Colgate resigned as university president and retreated with his wife, Rosie, to a cabin in Ward, Colorado. He decided to revisit an old interest: tornadoes. In his 1967 *Science* paper, he had urged scientists to launch instrumented probes into funnels. Well, why not do it himself? He asked the National Science Foundation for money to develop a prototype rocket. The NSF agreed on one condition: that the Federal Aviation Administration approve the rocket for flight. The FAA looked at Colgate's design for the rocket and said fine, go ahead. NSF awarded Colgate $60,000.

The "small rocket tornado probe" was the length of a cheerleader's baton and weighed less than a pound. The probe contained tiny weather instruments, powered by a 9-volt alkaline transistor battery. Colgate planned to strap several rockets to the underside of his plane's wings, then fire them into tornadoes. The instruments would measure air pressure and temperature within the funnel, plus any electrical activity. The probe's radio transmitter would send its measurements back to a minicomputer aboard the aircraft. Colgate developed numerous probes with the assistance of students and various friends in high-tech industries.

But he didn't want to test the rockets on a tornado, not right away. That was too risky. Instead, he headed to the Florida Keys, where he would test the rockets on waterspouts. He and a student lived in the Keys for two months, using Colgate's Cessna 210 to chase waterspouts. Colgate fired numerous rocket probes into the waterspouts, managing to hit "no more than a few." After a hard day of waterspout chasing, they relaxed at Key West's Half-Shell Raw Bar.

In spring 1980, Colgate decided he was ready to take on tornadoes. He shifted his base of operations to Norman, Oklahoma. Each morning he talked to meteorologists at NSSL to learn where storms were brewing. Then he flew there and surveyed the skies. From the wings of his Cessna hung a small arsenal of tornado rockets. Sometimes he'd fly day after day, never seeing a funnel. Typically "after two or three weeks, my wife, Rosie, would show up. Many times she'd stay at the airport in Norman, and stay there until midnight waiting for me to get back. It was hard on her." He chased again in the springs of 1981 and 1982.

May 22, 1981, was a busy day for tornadoes in western Oklahoma. Seven tornadoes touched down, ranging in intensity from F2 to F4. They hurt no one but caused scattered damage. The biggest twister was 1,200 yards wide, a monster that traveled 25 miles from the town of Binger to 12 miles north of Union City. It hurled cars and large oil tanks for a half mile, wrecked seven homes, and threw dead cattle into trees.

That day, Colgate encountered another twister 70 miles west of Oklahoma City. He fired four rockets at the funnel; he missed every time. The firings were recorded by an on-board Super 8 movie camera and two 16mm movie cameras, one on each wing. The film includes Colgate's narration. At the start of the film, the tornado appeared about a mile away. It was a grayish, ragged cone, whirring across the checkered farmlands. As Colgate spoke, he seemed to be panting slightly.

"We're going slowly towards it, but we see that it's somewhat unstable," he said, "and we're going to get as close as we can safely. It is *fantastic!*" Rain streaked across the window. Colgate had already used up half his movie film, but no matter: "I don't care if that movie goes all the way to the end, it's too fantastic a sight to miss. We've got some rain there, which is screwing up photography. No sign of any turbulence." The tornado was hundreds of feet wide, sheathed in dark mist, and appeared to be breaking up. He reached for the FIRE button and pressed it. The rocket spurted from its crib on the underside of one wing and blazed ahead, leaving a contrail behind. It shot past the twister. "We missed," Colgate groaned.

Now he had to move fast. The tornado was shrinking, a bad sign for several reasons. First, a narrower funnel is harder to hit. Also, as the funnel shrinks, angular momentum makes it rotate faster. The faster the twister rotates, the greater the chance it will tear the probe to bits. Colgate fired again: "One, two, three—fire!" Another rocket shot forth; another miss.

He decided to go for broke; he would move in closer. Now he was only a few thousand feet from the funnel. "All right—three, two, one: fire! There." The rocket shot straight toward the twister. Gleeful, Colgate started to shout, "Perfect!" But he didn't get past "Per—" The rocket veered away and vanished in the distance. He moaned. The day's chasing was finished, and all for naught.

The following January, Colgate described his work at the American Meteorological Society's 12th Conference on Severe Local Storms, in San Antonio. "The [rocket] equipment needs to be hardened and engineered to a significant degree," he said, "but we believe we have proved the feasibility of the probe, tactics, and launch platform [airplane] for future tornado work." He suggested firing future probes "from a land vehicle or a helicopter."

Colgate's third and final session was the spring of 1982. On May 19, he and a student, Dan Holden, soared in the skies over Pampa, Texas. Colgate flew a Centurion 210, designed to handle "near acrobatic stresses." On the ground, Rasmussen (then at Texas Tech) and other chasers pursued the Pampa tornadoes by car. About 5:30 P.M., Texas Tech's Tornado Intercept Program saw "striations" in the clouds "moving rapidly toward the wall cloud," as famed chaser Tim Marshall later wrote. Striations are grooves or channels in the clouds that indicate the direction of airflow. A few tornadoes came and went. "Then a large tornado with three sub-vortices developed a mile northwest of our location. . . . The tornado traveled northward through a plowed field picking up loose soil which changed the tornado to a dark red color. . . .

"By 7:05 P.M., the large, cyclonic tornado reversed its direction and moved southeastward toward our location. As a result, the team had to make a fast exit toward the east. . . ." The tornado hit the Pampa Industrial Park and smashed seven buildings.

Up in the air over Pampa, Colgate was having his own problems. He was chasing a twister when, suddenly, the plane hit a powerful downdraft. The aircraft reeled and dove toward the ground. He wrestled with the controls; Earth sped toward him like a wall. He turned the aircraft around moments before hitting the ground. Just before he righted the plane, he swears he saw "the television picture in someone's living room."

Shaken but determined, he flew on to the nearest tornado, "fired two or three rockets and turned tail." On the way back to Norman, a furious thunderstorm pummeled the plane. Colgate made an emergency landing in a field. He was shaken and upset. He would never chase another tornado.

CHAPTER 6

On the Road

Tornado studies are one of the few fields of scientific research where the amateur can make a significant contribution.

—Thomas P. Grazulis

A new subculture is sprouting across the Midwest: amateur tornado chasers. Mostly young and male, they race up and down the Midwest for days or weeks at a time, searching for the nastiest storms. Many chasers live off junk food and sleep in crummy motels. As the days pass, their cars fill with used videotapes, Coke cans, and Big Mac cartons. In short, they're having the time of their lives. And like any young people having a great time, they've made enemies.

The typical chaser is like Bob Henson: intelligent, level-headed, and mature. He'd never dream of driving onto private property to "get a better angle" for his video shot, or barging into a rural National

Weather Service office and using the computers without permission. But a minority of chasers do these things, and they've made life harder for those who don't.

Recently, the misfits earned a tongue-lashing from one of their heroes: Charles "Chuck" A. Doswell III of NSSL. He joined the first scientific chase teams in 1972. In March 1995, he was a star speaker at the first storm chasers' conference at a hotel in Norman, Oklahoma. Chasers and wannabe chasers packed the room (twice the expected number showed up). Doswell glared at the assemblage and warned: "If you choose to behave stupidly, there is nothing I can do about it. The highways are as open to you as they are to me.

"However, if you do something really dumb, and that action in some way jeopardizes my opportunities to chase storms, then I reserve the right to be upset with your behavior and to create as many obstacles to your continued stupid behavior as I can think of and get implemented."

He added, darkly: "If you ruin it for me, I'll come looking for you."

The perennial fear of chasers is that law-enforcement authorities will finally crack down and ban chasing (although it's unclear how a ban might be enforced). A ban could be triggered by a single dreadful incident: say, a chaser who, while pursuing a funnel cloud, slams into a school bus.

A major risk is chaser wannabes, people "who want to see a storm but have no idea what they're doing," says Gilbert Sebenste, a noted chaser from De Kalb, Illinois. He worries about the potential for a "major disaster." "If a tornado decides to take an abrupt turn—and they can do so at any time— everyone will be scrambling to turn their cars around, and a lot of people will die. That's one of the biggest fears that all the storm chasers have now. It has gotten so crowded out there that there is no room for error."

The first thing to remember is that amateur chasers serve a genuine scientific purpose. They are valuable partly because of their sheer numbers: They see and record tornadoes that might otherwise go unnoticed, and hence allow scientists to improve their understanding of tornado climatology—the frequency of tornadoes in different regions. Also, by spotting tornadoes, they enable forecasters to learn whether their forecast of a tornado came true or not. Forecasters can't improve their tornado forecasts unless they have a better idea what conditions are most likely to generate tornadoes. Amateurs' observations are partly responsible for forecasters' growing (and unsettling) realization that only a fraction of mesocyclones lead to tornadoes.

Storm chasing is one of the bravest expressions of scientific curiosity. A person who is curious about great literature doesn't risk his or her life by opening a book. An art lover doesn't fear death upon entering a museum. But storm chasers are so enthralled by one of nature's grandest events—the thunderstorm—that they risk death to observe it. To hostile outsiders, this impulse appears reckless, even psychopathological.

If that were so, then Benjamin Franklin belongs in the front ranks of psychopaths. He was America's first recorded storm chaser. In 1755 he, his son, and friends, including a Colonel Tasker, were riding horses in Maryland when

> we saw, in the vale below us, a small whirlwind beginning in the road and showing itself by the dust it raised and contained. It appeared in the form of a sugar loaf, spinning on its point, moving up the hill towards us, and enlarging as it came forward. When it passed by us, its smaller part near the ground appeared no bigger than a common barrel, but, widening upwards, it seemed at forty or fifty feet high to be twenty or thirty feet in diameter. The rest of the company stood looking after it, but, my curiosity being stronger, I followed it, riding close by its side, and observed its licking up in its progress all the dust that was under its smaller part.

Franklin's descendants now jam the highways every spring, angling for the best views of a supercell.

The first of them was David Hoadley. Professionally, he's a budget analyst for the Environmental Protection Agency. Privately, he's the father of modern storm chasing. Almost two decades ago, he founded *Storm Track* magazine, which remains (under a new editor, Tim Marshall) required reading for chasers and wannabes.

Sometime in the 1940s, young David Hoadley sat in a movie theater in Bismarck, North Dakota. Then he felt a hand touch his shoulder. It was his dad, who said: "There's a better show outside in the street." They walked outside. The Bismarck streets were a wreck—overturned trees, roofless homes, flooded avenues. A twister had struck town during the movie. Ever since, Hoadley has been hooked on storms.

Carson Eads has "the best-equipped chasemobile in Tornado Alley," according to the agenda at the Norman chasers' conference. In a slide show, he described how, while on the road, he uses a cellular phone, modem, and on-board computer to access the latest weather data. The van's TV antenna allows him to watch the Weather Channel anytime he likes. He also tows a portable Doppler radar behind the van. (The audience "oooohed" in envy.) An audience member asked Eads if he was guilty of technological "overkill." Eads grinned good-naturedly and replied, "Evidently I've got more money than I know what to do with."

Some chasers have turned chasing into cash. They sell their tornado videotapes to the Weather Channel or other outlets (one woman sold her tape to a beer company for a commercial). Others offer paid chase tours. An ad in *Storm Track* for the "Tornado

Alley Safari" says: "Come and enjoy the beauty and splendor of awesome skies, wild thunderstorms, and possible tornadoes. . . . One week/$1,050, two weeks $1,900. . . ."

Greed drives some chasers, complained Rich Thompson and Roger Edwards in a recent essay for *Storm Track*. They accused certain unnamed chasers of rushing to TV stations to sell their videotapes rather than remaining in the field and collaborating with other chasers. Commerce replaces camaraderie. "If chasers continue to promote this sport in this manner, the roads will eventually be clogged with so many 'yahoos,' and we will have no one to blame but ourselves."

Storm Track editor Tim Marshall and Randy Forey defended storm-chase capitalism. Storm chasing, they observed, is costly (the gas bills can be murder). Selling videos helps to recoup the costs. Besides, tornado videos educate the public. They added caustically that "the 'yahoos' are not from outside—they are from within—many are well-known, experienced chasers."

Most chasers became interested in weather at an early age. Bob Henson was seven when he saw a tornado watch on an Oklahoma City TV station. Afterward he cut and bent milk cartons into an anemometer, which he installed on his roof.

When Gilbert Sebenste was eight, he attended a picnic sponsored by his father's company in Illinois.

The weather forecasters had forecast sunshine. The day turned hot and humid. Young Gilbert knew enough about weather to know that heat and humidity presaged storms. "All of a sudden, I looked off to the west and saw this big huge mushroom [cloud] going up. . . . I ran back to the picnic and said, 'Dad, there's going to be a big storm.' " Soon the downburst hit: "All the prizes got blown out into the field—the bingo chips, all the cards. . . . I got under the table, my head under my hands. Everybody was screaming and yelling. It was general chaos. My dad put me on his shoulders and started running for the car. . . . He got almost knee deep in mud. That's the first time I ever heard my dad swear." When they arrived home, "my dad launched into a tirade against the weathermen." Gilbert agreed and thought, "Hey, I can do better than these clowns." He started making his own forecasts. Now he's both a prominent young storm chaser and a weather forecaster for a fair-size TV station in Illinois.

Recently Sebenste created the Storm Chaser Homepage on the World Wide Web. The Web is the Rodeo Drive of the global computer network known as the Internet. Anyone with a computer and modem (preferably a fast one, at least 14,400 baud) can access countless Web sites such as the Storm Chaser Homepage, which, despite its name, actually contains hundreds of pages of information. Juicy contents include high-resolution color photos of tornadoes, technical articles, and tornado experts' essays about tornado chasing and research. One can

learn much about tornadoes by pointing and click-
ing through the Storm Chaser Homepage—and
there is a great deal to learn. Storm chasing is not
for the ignorant.

One of the first things a young chaser learns is
that storms have their own geography. Some parts
of the storm are much more likely to generate tornadoes than others. The reasons for this are complicated, but are related to the internal airflow in a
supercell as it moves from southwest to northeast
(the usual path of U.S. storms). Experienced chasers
head for the storm's rain-free southwest quadrant,
where (in the Midwestern United States) a tornado
is most likely to form. They keep their eyes peeled
for a wall cloud—the rotating cloud (sometimes
shaped like a hockey puck or a wedge) that drops
from the base of the thundercloud. When they see a
wall cloud, they try to situate themselves southeast
of it, partly to watch it approach from the west.
(That lengthens their viewing time, just as one situ-
ates oneself ahead of a parade to enjoy it for a longer
time.) A southeastern position is also good because,
there, a chaser's view is less likely to be obscured by
rain and hail, which usually fall on the northern side
of the storm. And there's a third reason for staying
to the southeast: to get the best photos and video
coverage. Because most tornadoes occur in the late
afternoon or early evening, a southeastern position
is ideal because the clouds will contrast dramati-
cally with the bright western sky, where the sun sets.

This writer visited Sebenste at Northern Illinois University in De Kalb. There Sebenste regularly updates the Storm Chaser Homepage at a computer workstation in the meteorology department. He's bubbly and extremely friendly, a tall, slender young man with short dark hair and dark-rimmed glasses. On the wall is a photo of a previous TV weather forecaster who made it big, David Letterman. Sebenste switched on the computer and signed on to the Storm Chaser Homepage. He clicked the mouse to show a page about one of his own recent tornado chases.

"It's been a very busy year. We've had a record number of tornadoes in Illinois—58 so far. It's the best year we've had since 1990 or '91. 1991, '92, '93, and '94 were just *awful*. . . . Every year is different and nobody knows why." Personally, he suspects the jet stream, that meandering river of high-altitude, high-speed air. Sometimes the jet stream diverts severe weather north or south of Great Lakes states such as Illinois, depriving him of the storms he loves.

Chasing is fun "for about three minutes out of the year. Storm chasing requires an incredible amount of patience and understanding. It can best be described as 'hurry up and wait.' You go to where the tornadoes are supposed to be and wait—hours and hours and hours. You'll be sitting under the blue sky, getting a nice tan, and that's all you'll see for the rest of day." But when a tornado touches down, "it's incredible fun and excitement. . . . You get an appreciation for what goes on in Mother Nature—appreciation that you just can't get in the class-room."

Just down the road from Sebenste is the College of Du Page in Du Page, Illinois. Professor Paul Sirvatka teaches an undergraduate class on storm chasing. Every spring he takes several dozen students on chases across the Midwest. The class helps his students visualize weather phenomena in "three dimensions," which is easier to appreciate in the field than in the classroom, he explains. He has taken students within a mile of a tornado. "We've been in some fairly hairy situations—we really thought the vans were about to tip over—but nothing I would consider life-threatening.

"This year was one of the worst—two trips, two busts. We spent most of the time sightseeing in Colorado and South Dakota, and there was just *nothing* happening in the sky. Then we came back, and while driving through Illinois, we got three tornadoes just outside of Springfield!"

Kim Ball joined that trip. She's a mother, thin and blond; she recently returned to school to get her degree in computer science. She says one of the Illinois tornadoes resembled a huge, V-shaped wedge. "Our eyes were popping out. We saw trucks and cars that had flipped over."

When this writer told her she was the first female chaser he had met, she laughed. "I've been on chases where there were three or four women, and sometimes it was almost 50-50 male and female. But when it comes to meteorology majors, there're definitely more men than women."

CHAPTER 7

The White Plague and Global Warming

In early 1995, on three separate occasions, the "white plague" struck the Dallas-Fort Worth area of Texas. The white plague is farmers' nickname for hail. On March 25, April 29, and May 5, more than a billion dollars in damage occurred as hailstones plunged from the sky. The hail measured up to five inches wide and wrecked cars and aircraft on the ground. On the evening of May 5, about 10,000 people attended an arts and crafts fair in Fort Worth. Baseball-size hail began falling. "Parents cowered over their children as fist-size stones propelled at 80 mph hit them in the backs, necks, heads, and arms, causing three-inch welts," storm chaser Tim Marshall reported. Car windows exploded, spraying glass on the occupants. Incredibly, no one died.

Hailstones are dramatic evidence of the strength of thunderstorm updrafts. Blowing at hundreds of miles per hour, these winds shoot water droplets several miles high, where they freeze and fall back toward Earth. On the descent, the ice pellets gather more water, then are blown upward again, where they refreeze, fall again, rise again, over and over. Gradually they acquire onion-like layers of ice—sometimes dozens of layers. Eventually they grow heavy enough to plunge all the way to the ground. Some hailstorms smash barns and wreck cars and tractors; some slaughter cattle; some kill people.

In the 1940s, the scientist Albert K. Showalter suggested that hail triggered tornadoes. Others have proposed similar theories. In 1953, Colonel Rollin H. Mayer and Fritz O. Rossmann planned to destroy tornadoes with guided missiles. They based the plan on Rossmann's theory that tornadoes were spawned by cold downdrafts generated by hailstones. As hail falls, Rossmann said, it cools the air and drags it to Earth. Critics cited an obvious flaw in the theory: Tornadoes tend to form in the part of the storm where there isn't hail or rain!

❋

Recent research on hail hints that we'll see more tornadoes in the future. It's just a hint—but a tantalizing one.

Scientists are increasingly worried about global

warming, also known as the greenhouse effect. The burning of fossil fuels (from cars, industries, etc.) injects carbon dioxide gas into the atmosphere. The gas traps infrared heat (as a greenhouse traps solar heat) generated by solar radiation. Many scientists think this heat-trapping raises the planetary temperature.

The planet's average temperature has risen for about a century. Global warming may partly explain why mountain glaciers are shrinking. A century ago the naturalist John Muir sketched glaciers in the mountains of Yosemite. Today those glaciers are considerably smaller because of local (and perhaps global) warming. Another possible sign of global warming is recent satellite observations, which indicate the global sea level is rising. Conceivably, global warming could elevate sea level by melting polar ice.

Would global warming worsen severe storms such as hurricanes, thunderstorms, hailstorms, and tornadoes? Scientists are starting to study this exciting question. Research by meteorology Professor Kerry A. Emanuel at MIT suggests that warming would breed more hurricanes. That's worth noting because many hurricanes breed tornadoes. The record for hurricane-bred twisters is held by Hurricane Beulah, which struck Texas in September 1967 and may have caused as many as 141 tornadoes.

Even if global warming doesn't get out of hand, severe tornadoes may become more frequent in the next few decades. Grazulis, the tornado climatologist who advised the Nuclear Regulatory Commission, says that in the 1980s, the annual number of "violent" tornadoes averaged six per year. "The 1980s," he says, "were clearly a low period in violent tornado activity. . . . The possibility of an increase in violent activity, and a corresponding increase in deaths, over the next decade or two is a real one."

Why would the number of violent tornadoes vary from decade to decade? No one knows. Perhaps it has something to do with short-term climate changes, such as "El Niño," a quasi-cyclical warming of Pacific waters that affects global climate. Or perhaps it's just the result of natural atmospheric variance, as unpredictable as a gambler's lucky streak.

CHAPTER 8

Putting Tornadoes to Work

Can we put tornadoes to use? Over the decades, a number of scholars have speculated about creating or simulating tornadoes for a variety of purposes, ranging from military applications to energy production.

Humans noticed decades (perhaps centuries) ago that they could create artificial tornadoes. Spinning columns of air form over large bonfires, as ancient peoples may well have observed. They may also have seen funnels associated with forest fires or volcanic eruptions. Similar phenomena are seen today: Few sights are more terrifying to a firefighter in a forest than a "fire whirlwind."

Scientists have generated fire vortices for research

purposes. The world's ultimate tornado machine is outdoors and located in the Pyrenees Mountains of southwestern France. John Snow has worked with scientists there to generate artificial tornadoes from giant oil fires. "Meteotron" has 105 fuel oil burners that create the equivalent of a billion watts of energy—a gigawatt, as much as a large nuclear power plant. The father-son team of Henri and Jean Dessens began working there in the 1960s, using the facility to generate artificial cumulus clouds and tornado-like vortices. Some vortices extended hundreds of feet into the sky.

In the 1970s, during the global energy crisis, some experts speculated about novel energy schemes that would tap power from thunderstorms or tornado-like vortices. W. George N. Slinn of Battelle Pacific Northwest Laboratories suggested exploiting cloud power by funneling waste heat from nuclear power plants into the air. This would, he said, form thunderstorms that, in turn, would drop rain that could feed hydroelectric plants. Another scheme was proposed by James Yen of Grumman Aerospace Corporation, who advocated building enclosed wind generators that would suck in outside air and, by exploiting the law of angular momentum, create a narrow, low-pressure, rotating column of air—a vortex, akin to a tornado. The wind could then be used to drive a dynamo and produce electricity.

Perhaps the most astonishing human-created tornadoes—outside of warfare—resulted from an industrial catastrophe in 1926. San Luis Obispo is a charming college town nestled in the mountains of central California, not far from the Pacific. At 7:35 A.M., April 7, a bolt of lightning struck oil reservoirs at a tank farm operated by Union Oil Company, 2.5 miles south of town. The tanks detonated. The shock wave smashed windows all over town; people flooded into the streets, thinking an earthquake had hit. The burning tanks "threw out an immense quantity of hot, burning oil which spread with remarkable rapidity over an area . . . [of] about 900 acres," a witness later wrote. "The flames leaped seemingly a thousand feet in the air. . . . At the same time violent whirlwinds began to form over the fire." Apparently a northwest wind from a passing storm caused wind shear, forcing the rising, scalding air to rotate. The faster it rotated, the more it tightened into a neat, whirling column (angular momentum at work). The human-created twister "left the vicinity . . . and traveling east-northeast about 1,000 yards picked up the Seeber cottage, just outside the tank farm, lifting it several feet in the air and carrying it about 150 feet north, where it was dropped in a field, a total wreck.

Scientists can *start* tornadoes, yet they still don't know how to stop them. Nor do they know how to forecast them (with much reliability, anyway), or even how to penetrate them reliably with scientific instruments.

Still, the future beckons. Researchers are working to overcome these and other challenges, via futuristic technologies—virtual reality, supercomputers, and space satellites.

CHAPTER 9

No Man's Land

Where will the future take tornado science? Can tornado forecasts be improved? How will twenty-first century scientists simulate, chase, and explore these storms? Will the old dream of tornado modification be revived?

And in the meantime, what can you—as an individual and a citizen—do to protect yourself, your family, and your community against these cruelest of tempests?

This writer slid the virtual reality helmet over his head. Through its spectacles he saw, in the distance, a bright, boiling thundercloud. He pressed a button on a baton-shaped control stick in his hand. Suddenly, he shot into the interior of the storm. Within the immense cloud, he floated from its broad, flat base to its anvil-shaped top. He saw updrafts, represented by swirls of glowing green dots. The dots zipped past him like rocket-powered fireflies. Beneath him, downdrafts flushed from the storm's bottom and swept across the countryside. He could trigger a new updraft or downdraft just by pressing the button. He felt like the ancient god Zeus, lord of lightning: He could tell a thundercloud what to do.

A male voice interrupted his reverie: "Does the helmet fit okay?" asked Professor Bob Wilhelmson. Then the writer remembered that he wasn't soaring through a storm 10,000 feet above Earth. Rather, he was standing in a virtual reality cage at the University of Illinois.

The university is a scientific oasis in Urbana-Champaign, amid the corn country of downstate Illinois, the eastern edge of Tornado Alley. Here, Wilhelmson and other scientists are using supercomputers to simulate tornadoes and other severe weather. Despite its geographical isolation, the campus has always been on the cutting edge of computer science. (According to the science-fiction film *2001*, it's where the villainous computer HAL 9000 was born.) Campus scientists use supercomputers to simulate—in gorgeous color—phenomena such as exploding stars, collapsing black holes, the flow of subterranean oil, and the wiggle of electrons moving within enzymes. Almost two decades ago, Wilhelmson used an earlier supercomputer—pokey by today's standards—to simulate a thunderstorm. Now he's refining the model and adding a thunderstorm's meanest weapon: a tornado. The supercomputer crunches night and day. Its circuits are cooled by a built-in air conditioner, lest they overheat.

Perhaps some day in the dim future it will be possible to advance the computations faster than the weather advances and at a cost less than the saving to mankind due to the information gained. But that is a dream.

—Lewis Fry Richardson (1922)

It was a dream in 1922, but it isn't anymore. Computers are now essential tools in meteorology. They're vital both for daily weather forecasts and sophisticated simulations such as Wilhelmson's. Researchers at NSSL and elsewhere have developed algorithms—computer programs—that scan Doppler radar screens. The algorithms check for warning signs of severe storms such as tornadoes, hailstorms, and high winds. For example, scientists are testing a new algorithm that scans Doppler radar screens and looks for mesocyclones. The mesocyclones are represented by adjacent regions of different colors, such as red and green, on the screen. Green regions mark winds blowing toward the radar, the red winds blowing away. The algorithm is so good that it heralds a "paradigm shift" in such technology, says a recent paper by Greg Stumpf, Caren Marzban, and Erik Rasmussen. In a series of tests, the algorithm correctly identified 38 out of 49 (78 percent) mesocyclones on radar screens. Other algorithms monitor the screens for hail, high winds, and other severe weather. Such algorithms could save future forecasters the task of constantly monitoring radar screens.

Could future computers *replace* human forecasters? Humans have feared losing their jobs to machines since the dawn of the Industrial Revolution. Machines have already replaced humans in most jobs based on raw strength and many that depend on physical dexterity. Will twenty-first-century computers eliminate most jobs based on brainpower as well? Meteorology is a classic brainpower career. Harold Brooks of NSSL recently wrote a provocative essay, ominously titled "The Possible Future Role of Humans in Weather Forecasting."

Forecasters, he says, are essential for forecasting "extremely difficult" phenomena such as convection (which spawns thunderstorms and tornadoes). "Doing it well requires a knowledge of a vast range of scales of motion and behavior in the atmosphere. Human skills of pattern recognition and information processing should continue to be critical."

The more we learn about tornadoes, the more complicated they look. Decades ago, scientists assumed there was one basic type of tornado. But chase teams have discovered beyond doubt that there are at least several types. Some descend from supercell thunderstorms with mesocyclones; some don't. Supercells generate the most violent twisters, but other atmospheric events produce "landspouts," "gust-nadoes," and "mountainadoes," which can also cause significant harm.

That complexity could undermine high hopes for the nation's newest defense against tornadoes: NEXRAD, a network of 160 Doppler radar units (also called WSR-88Ds). They measure the speed of winds, based on frequency shifts in radar reflections from precipitation particles blown by those winds. Meteorologists say NEXRAD radar will greatly enhance their ability to detect atmospheric circulation associated with tornadoes. The radar will also detect gust fronts, strong updrafts that may generate severe hail, and deadly downbursts and microbursts that threaten both aircraft and surface structures.

If many or most tornadoes form at low altitudes, then NEXRAD may be less effective than originally hoped, for a simple physical reason: the Earth is round. You may have watched boats disappear over the horizon, that is, over the curve of the planetary surface. That same curvature limits the range of a NEXRAD radar: It can't see objects (such as thunderstorms) below the horizon. That means it can't scan the lower sections of a distant thunderstorm. Doswell says that if a storm is more than a few tens of miles from the radar, Earth's curvature will "virtually preclude" detection of tornadic radar signals from low altitudes in the storm.

Because a minority of mesocyclones lead to tornadoes, forecasters who issue warnings every time their Doppler radar detects a mesocyclone will issue mostly false alarms. False alarms are bad because they feed what one might call the "boy cries wolf" effect: The more false alarms, the less likely the public will trust tornado watches. Such distrust could lead to countless deaths and injuries.

In short, Doppler radar won't solve tornado forecasters' problems. Forecasters should continue to use other ways to forecast tornadoes. For example, forecasters can monitor breaks in power lines that may be caused by twisters. They can also stay in contact with spotter groups, whose thousands of volunteers watch the skies for twisters during tornado season.

In other words: Radar is a great tool, but the best tornado detection device is still the human eye. Computers are great, but they won't replace human forecasters for a long time.

Still, hope springs eternal. . . . Better tornado forecasts may eventually come from above—from outer space.

A new space satellite monitors lightning from space. The satellite may help scientists answer an old question: Do tornadic storms generate unusual amounts or types of lightning? And if so, could they use lightning detectors on the ground or in space to improve tornado warnings?

In chapter 4, this writer talked about Bernard Vonnegut's idea that electricity generates tornadoes. That idea has largely fallen by the wayside. Still, some scientists suspect that tornadic storms tend to generate remarkably intense lightning (especially positive cloud-to-ground bolts) for reasons unrelated to the tornado itself. In the early 1950s, Professor Herbert L. Jones of Oklahoma A & M College claimed that tornadic storms emit much more high-frequency electrical signals (called sferics, after *atmospherics*) than ordinary tornadic storms. Inspired, entrepreneurs marketed tornado detectors— alarms that sounded if they detected a surge in the local electrical field. In the 1970s, scientists investigated claims that tornadic storms' electrical activity caused a TV set tuned to channel 2 to glow brightly. Popular magazines ran articles explaining how to turn a TV set into a tornado monitor during a severe storm. Nowadays, the nicest thing one can say about tornado detectors is that they are unproven and probably generate numerous false alarms.

NASA launched the Optical Transient Detector (OTD) satellite on April 3, 1995. It monitors lightning flashes from orbit in space. On April 17, the OTD passed over a violent storm in Oklahoma. The instrument detected a surge in the number of lightning bolts, to more than 60 per second. About a minute later, ground observers saw a tornado touch down. NASA claimed OTD offers "the possibility of identifying the formation of tornadoes and severe storms from space."

Scientists seek other ways to use satellites to distinguish between thunderstorms that will drop tornadoes and those that won't. Tall, severe thunderstorms have powerful updrafts that punch through the cloud's icy roof and into the lower part of the stratosphere. These dome-shaped protrusions are called overshooting tops. From space satellites, overshooting tops resemble warts on smooth skin. Fujita and others have explored possible links between overshooting tops and the time of a tornado touchdown. Scientists also study possible connections between tornadoes and other cloud top features, such as mysterious V-shaped cold spots.

NASA began launching a new series of weather satellites in 1994. The space agency launched GOES-8 (Geostationary Operational Environmental Satellite) from Cape Canaveral aboard an Atlas Centaur rocket on April 13, 1994. The $220-million, 22,000-mile-high probe is geostationary because it stays above the same point on Earth—75 degrees west longitude, off the east coast of the United States. The new satellites can "zoom in on a significant weather event every five minutes while continuing to provide overall coverage," NOAA officials say. These "eyes in space" could prove invaluable for monitoring severe storms such as tornadoes, hurricanes, flash floods, and hail storms.

Researchers are studying ways to strengthen homes and other buildings against tornadoes. Many buildings could survive tornadoes if better built, say scientists at Texas Tech's Institute for Disaster Research (IDR). Unfortunately, structural engineers have as much trouble persuading people in Tornado Alley to spend several hundred dollars making their homes tornado-resistant as they have persuading Californians to make their homes earthquake-resistant. "It won't happen to me" is the usual excuse.

Since 1987 the insurance industry has paid a fortune for windstorm damages. In response, the industry is pressuring states to tighten building codes. It's an uphill battle: Politically powerful homebuilders associations oppose any new regulations.

At IDR, scientists simulate tornado damage by using a cannon to fire high-speed projectiles (lumber, pipes, etc.) at walls. In the 1970s, IDR scientists concluded that even the worst tornado damage could be caused by winds as weak as 275 mph. Their research has helped building engineers develop new structural engineering codes for wind-resistant buildings.

"Some structures—such as nuclear power plants—need complete protection from tornadoes regardless of the high costs of design and construction. Public facilities also need protection, but local governments rarely have the necessary funds," said architect Harold W. Harris and IDR's Kishor C. Mehta and James R. McDonald in a 1992 article for *Civil Engineering* magazine. "Yet a fairly high degree of defense is available for a minimal amount of money." They urge businesses and schools to establish enhanced tornado protective areas (ETPAs), where people can safely hide during a tornado. The ETPA should be on the same floor as its occupants: "Moving several hundred students up or down stairs is time-consuming." A building's interior may be safe even if it wasn't designed for tornadoes. For example, a Xenia, Ohio, high school was "virtually destroyed" by a tornado in 1974. Yet the first-floor hallway was undamaged.

Old buildings are especially vulnerable, particularly those with unreinforced masonry. Vulnerable masonry can be reinforced by inserting steel rods into the walls. Special frames and trusses also enhance building stability.

Facilities in tornado-prone areas may prefer to buy a dedicated tornado shelter rather than to retrofit their existing plant. One of the world's top particle physics laboratories is Fermi National Accelerator Laboratory (Fermilab) in rural Batavia, Illinois, west of Chicago. Recently, lab officials unveiled what they claim is the world's strongest above-ground tornado shelter. Shaped like a loaf of French bread, the above-ground shelter can hold several dozen people. Its walls are steel-reinforced precast concrete. North Star Chicago Precast of Naperville, Illinois, made it and markets similar shelters. Other firms sell shelters as small as in-home units for families. The house may collapse, but the shelter will (in theory) remain intact.

Steel-frame homes are an intriguing new option. An estimated 50,000 steel-frame homes were built in the United States in 1995 (about 4 percent of the total)—100 times as many as in 1992. Builders claim that well-built steel-frame homes resist high winds and earthquakes (not to mention termites!) They cost slightly more than wood-frame homes. The American Iron & Steel Institute hopes to seize 25 percent of the new-home market by 1999.

What do you do if you see a tornado approaching?

First, be aware of an important distinction:

(1) A "tornado watch" means a tornado *might* appear but hasn't been seen yet.

(2) A "tornado warning" means a tornado has been detected. Head for shelter immediately. If you are driving, head for a safe place.

During a tornado watch, turn on a radio or TV and listen for further advisories. Protect valuables—for example, move your car into the garage. Otherwise the tornado might turn it into a missile and hurl it into your home or someone else's.

If you have time, move other potential missiles outside your home (lawn furniture, lawnmowers, pink flamingoes, etc.) indoors.

If you hear sirens, they mean you should stay indoors and take cover.

However, don't wait to hear warning sirens before you head for shelter. Sirens usually *don't* wail before a tornado hits. (Remember Barneveld!)

Do NOT get into your car to flee the area! Research shows that motorists are much more likely to be killed or injured than people who stay at home. "Do not attempt to outdrive a tornado," warns the Federal Emergency Management Agency. "They are erratic and move swiftly."

Do NOT run around your home to open windows! Experts no longer believe this is a good way to protect your home. Until about 1980, emergency officials believed that buildings exploded from internal air pressure as the low-pressure tornado funnel passed overhead. Then researchers at the Institute for Disaster Research studied building damage in detail and concluded building damage was caused by high winds, not by explosions. Indeed, you might *increase* the risk of damage by opening windows, which admits high winds that could accumulate in the center of the house, rise, and shove the roof off! Also, if you run around opening windows, you risk being hit by flying glass and other debris.

Another myth is that the southwestern part of a building is always the safest place. There may be safer spots.

If you're in a mobile home during a tornado warning, leave and head for a safe structure or low, protected ground. The jokes about trailer parks being magnets for tornadoes are based on tragic truth: Trailers are too flimsy to withstand high winds.

If a tornado approaches, head for the basement and hide under a sturdy structure (such as a heavy table or workbench). If you don't have a basement, then hide in a small interior room—say, a bathroom or closet.

Avoid windows (they may shatter) and outside walls (they may collapse).

Avoid big open rooms such as gymnasiums and auditoriums. They tend to collapse. If you're in a shopping mall, find the center of the building and go to the lowest level. (Do *not* go to your parked car!) Again, avoid windows and big, open rooms.

If a tornado is near and you're in a car, get out of the vehicle and lie down in a ravine, ditch, culvert, or other low area. Place your hands behind the back of your head and neck to avoid neck injury. If you're in a low area, keep an eye out for flash floods.

After the tornado has struck, check for gas leaks; know how to turn off your utilities if necessary. When you leave the building, watch out for fallen electrical lines and broken glass. It wouldn't hurt to have a fire extinguisher nearby. (Be sure that you know how to use it—and that it hasn't passed its expiration date!)

The best safety precautions are those taken long before the tornado hits. To protect yourself, your family, and your neighbors, you might consider:

—Practicing "disaster drills" with your family.

—Stocking emergency supplies in advance. These include a flashlight (along with a fresh, unopened pack of batteries), candles (with matches in a waterproof container), first-aid items (again, in a waterproof container), and a transistor radio.

—Joining a local tornado spotter's group. For details, call your local emergency preparedness office.

—Obtaining a copy of *Are You Ready?*, FEMA's comprehensive guide to preparedness for every conceivable major disaster from tornadoes to earthquakes to hurricanes to hazardous materials spills.

If you live in a trailer park, find out where your trailer park's emergency shelter is located—if it has one. If it doesn't, ask the park manager to install one. Your outspokenness may end up saving more lives than your own. Make sure the shelter is accessible to people who are frail, handicapped, or need medical assistance.

For children, NOAA and FEMA offer a cartoon-filled brochure called "Owlie Skywarn's Weather Book."

Spanish-language tornado warning brochures are available from NOAA, the American Red Cross, and FEMA. The Spanish-speaking population of the United States is rising, especially in tornado-prone border states. If you have neighbors who are new to the United States and some of them are still learning English, you would be doing them a favor by bringing these brochures to their attention, or by posting them at a central location (say, a community center or place of worship).

The sky is literally the limit for tornado chasers. One day astronauts may pursue tornadoes across the orange-red sands of Mars. Space scientists who study close-up photos of Mars have noted bright glows and mysterious dark trails on the planetary surface. The bright glows, they say, are dust devils. The trails may be tornado tracks, etched in the rust-colored soil by passing families of twisters.

The future is bright for Earth-based tornado chasers, too. VORTEX is over, but the scientists have gathered mountains of data that they'll spend years analyzing. Smaller versions of VORTEX may be held in coming years—if federal funds hold out.

New technologies may aid vortex chasers. Joseph Golden of NOAA thinks helicopters might become the choice chase vehicle of tomorrow. They're unhampered by roads and can travel at top speed. In 1993, on an expedition funded by the National Geographic Society, he flew in a helicopter past waterspouts in the Florida Keys. He also speculates about turning speedboats (with weather instruments) into chase vehicles for waterspout research.

A priority of future research should be the launching of instrumented probes into funnels, perhaps with small rockets (à la Stirling Colgate) or remotely controlled small airplanes. The plane couldn't survive a flight into the funnel, but a missile might. Maybe scientists could acquire a few military surplus "smart" missiles, similar to those used in the Gulf War, and outfit them with video cameras and weather instruments. There are worse ways to beat swords into plowshares, anyway.

One imagines what the little rocket might see as it plunges through the hurricane-force wall of the twister and, guided by remote control, soars up and down the funnel, measuring wind speeds and temperatures. Entire fleets of rockets might be launched into tornadoes, to record sights never before seen.

And who can say that someday, a human might not follow them? Only a fool would deliberately attempt to enter a tornado, of course. But foolhardiness is the consistent trait of all pioneers. Most chasers are young; and like most young people, they believe they're going to live forever. Sooner or later, against all common sense, by some means we can only dimly imagine, one of them will likely attempt the impossible—to deliberately enter a tornado.

It would be an insane act, of course. So was Lindbergh's flight across the Atlantic.

Tornado watcher Anton Seimon is about as young now as the white-haired Robert Davies-Jones was a quarter of a century ago, when scientific chasing was born. Over that time chasers have changed our view of tornadoes. What sights will they see over the *next* twenty-five years? The interior of the tornado remains as remote, as little understood, as the surface of Pluto. Will it remain forever so? "I wouldn't be surprised," Seimon said with a faraway sound in his voice, "if in the next ten years, someone survives a trip into that no man's land with a video camera."

AFTERWORD

The University of Illinois's virtual reality thunderstorm is crude compared to the tornadoes of the film *Twister*. *Twister*'s tornadoes make a quantum leap forward in the techniques of digital moviemaking. They also foretell the future of film: Tomorrow's moviemakers will depict on screen *anything* that the mind can imagine.

Until now, the most celebrated computer-generated film images involved the simulation of objects with geometric or continuous surfaces. Classic examples include *Terminator 2*'s murderous linoleum floor, which rises and transforms into a cyborg who kills a cop; and the watery pseudopod in *The Abyss*, which emerges, like a long, translucent worm, from a sunken spaceship and slithers toward a female scientist, then changes shape to imitate her facial expressions.

But *Twister* involves a radically different type of digital effect. A tornado is not a single object with an unbroken surface. Rather, it is a constantly moving *swarm* of objects—billions of them. In nature, a tornado is a vortex of high-speed wind—moving air—that is, by itself, invisible. (You can't see air.) What makes the tornado visible is the objects that swirl around it: water droplets (the cloudlike condensation funnel that sheathes the vortex), dust particles, and larger chunks of debris such as cows, cars, and roofs. These objects are, in effect, the tornado's "clothes" that make it visible to the naked eye.

How could computer moviemakers simulate such a complex, high-speed maelstrom of objects? The answer is that initially they weren't sure they could. Before giving *Twister* the go-ahead, executive producer Steven Spielberg asked special effects experts at Industrial Light & Magic (ILM) in Marin County, California—where *Jurassic Park*'s digital dinosaurs were born—to demonstrate that they could create realistic-looking tornadoes on computer screens. The ILM wizards made a test film by putting a small movie crew in the back of a car and filming the driver as he drove toward a building. Then they digitized the images and used computer techniques to "paint" a tornado in the distance as it tore a building to bits, then hurled another vehicle at his windshield. The results were stunning—as convincing as a documentary film on tornadoes.

"*Twister* couldn't have been made without digital effects," director Jan De Bont declares.

Twister depicts a wild menagerie of tornadoes, as diverse in shape and size as real-life twisters. Some are serpentine, whitish funnels that snake elegantly over a body of water. One is a menacing, mud-brown torrent that almost kills the film's heroes, tornado chasers Jo and Bill Harding (played by Helen Hunt and Bill Paxton), then steals Jo's car. And yet another is a hellish funnel into whose interior Jo and Bill gaze at the film's climax.

The actors performed on location, shooting in Oklahoma and Iowa in the first half of 1995. Then the footage was sent to ILM, where tornadoes were digitally added to the footage.

The most famous tornado movie is, of course, *The Wizard of Oz* (1939). The film was directed by Victor Fleming and starred Judy Garland as Dorothy, the Kansas farm girl who, with her Scotch terrier, Toto, travels aboard a twister to the marvelous land of Oz. *The Wizard of Oz*'s tornado—a dark, writhing funnel—is one of the unforgettable images of filmdom. The tornado is, in fact, a 35-foot-long muslin windsock.

Oz's tornado is still wondrous to behold. But scientifically speaking, it is—to put it politely—somewhat idealized. In reality, many tornadoes lack the *Oz* funnel's smooth, sinuous shape. Also, very few whip back and forth so elegantly, like bullwhips. Since the early 1980s, many Americans have seen close-up videotapes of real tornadoes on TV; they've learned that many twisters are, in fact, complex and highly unstable objects. Many look less like smooth funnels than ragtag assemblies of individual clouds.

Such public awareness put pressure on *Twister*'s makers because "we're having to duplicate nature," says producer Kathleen Kennedy. But there was no practical way to simulate a modern-looking tornado with a physical model like *Oz*'s wind-sock. Ordinary animation was out of the question, too. Some films have shown twisters that were actually animated cartoons superimposed on live-action shots; and unfortunately, they *look* like cartoons. In short, digital technology offered the only hope for creating realistic-looking tornado images that would satisfy the savviest tornado buffs.

To demonstrate digital construction of a tornado, ILM visual effects supervisor Stefen Fangmeir switched on his Silicon Graphics computer workstation. A skeletal, cartoon-like outline of a tornado appeared on the screen. "It looks like a giant caterpillar," Fangmeir said, moving the mouse to manipulate the tornado. It resembled a wire-mesh outline of a funnel with blue points to mark different positions. The funnel was situated on a larger wire-mesh grid that represented the terrain—specifically, a drainage ditch where Jo and Bill have fled for safety. "The animator controls the shape of the tornado and the rate at which it moves across the terrain."

Next step: to give the skeletal tornado a realistic-looking texture—in effect, to give it "skin." Most tornadoes' surfaces appear rough, not smooth. How can digital artists mimic that roughness without wasting months digitally "painting" each pixel on the computer screen? ILM artists create mathematical programs that automatically generate rough-looking fractal (fractional dimension) surfaces. By altering the data inputted in the program, they can vary the amount of roughness on an object. (Back in the 1980s, moviemakers began using fractal mathematics to create realistically rough-looking surfaces, such as mountainsides. A noted example is the Genesis Planet created for one of the *Star Trek* films.) "Fairly complex algorithms [computerized mathematical programs] allow us to do this. Of course," Fangmeir adds with a smile, "we write completely different algorithms for dinosaurs."

With further computer tinkering, they can add colors (for example, a dirt-brown shade), sprinkle flying debris around the funnel, and make it rotate. The result is an astonishingly realistic-looking tornado. To generate such images requires gigabytes—billions of bytes—of computer disk space, as much as one can store in dozens of small personal computers.

Digital techniques also allowed the digital artists to synchronize the tornado's motion, frame by frame, with the constant bouncing and jumping of the camera. There's a lot of bouncing in this movie as Jo and Bill race in their truck across the countryside or flee by foot from a twister. In old-time Hollywood, filmmakers enjoyed the luxury of a static camera: It sat still and filmed a scene while actors moved in front of it. But nowadays, bouncing camera motion (the hand-held camera look) is a staple of action films; audiences *expect* it. A bouncing screen image contributes to the viewers' sense of realism and replicates what their eyes would actually see—their field of view—if they were *with* Jo and Bill on a chase. So ILM digital artists couldn't simply "paint" a tornado on a screen; rather they had to model the entire scene three-dimensionally in a computer to ensure that the tornado retained the correct position as the camera jiggled around.

Another digital effect is motion blur. In early science-fiction films, dinosaur puppets were animated frame by frame, which gave their motion a jerky look. In the real world, objects move continuously, and the faster they move, the more the eye perceives their motion as blurred. So by creating artificial blur, digital experts enhance the realism of a moving digital object. They create the blur by using the computer to spread out the moving object's image. Motion blur was a key factor in contributing to the verisimilitude of *Jurassic Park*'s dinosaurs. (If you take a videotape of the film, stick it in your VCR, and freeze-frame it during a special effects scene, you'll see that individual components—say, one of the *Tyrannosaurus rex*'s arms—are blurred.) Likewise in *Twister*, swarms of debris (all computer generated) are motion-blurred to enhance their realism.

Fangmeir showed how ILM digital artists designed a cow that, in one memorable scene, flies past the window of Jo and Bill's truck. Originally the cow was a zebra used in the recent Robin Williams fantasy movie *Jumanji*. Via computer techniques, they transformed the zebra into a cow. Nowadays, the cow effect is a "rather run of the mill" effect for digital artists, Fangmeir says. Even so, it's time-consuming; he estimated that digital artists had to work the equivalent of a few man-months to create the flying cow. The flying cow effect is funny and, best of all (visual effects producer Kim Bromley notes), the Humane Society need not worry: No cows (or other animals) were harmed in the making of this film—only digital ones.

Science-fiction movies are littered with almost-invisible "jokes." For example, during the making of the *Star Wars* trilogy, a model maker glued a tiny replica of San Francisco's pyramidal Transamerica Building on the side of a giant starship. Likewise, in *Twister*, effects experts created whimsical digital images of tornado-blown debris—such as a plastic pink flamingo from someone's lawn. "One of the modelers' nicknames is Edsel," Bromley said, "so he modeled a grille from an Edsel car and made it into a piece of debris."

In January 1996, De Bont, the director, sat in a darkened room filled with ILM staffers and examined a video playout of their latest handiwork. The video screen showed the same short scene over and over. The scene started with an image of the sky taken from a camera aboard a truck; a slender, grayish tornado lurks in the distance. Then the camera pans to the left, past a damaged tractor—one of its wheels is still spinning following its encounter with the twister. The scene ends with the anxious face of the driver, Bill Harding's fiancée, Melissa Reeves, played by Jami Gertz. Reeves is *Twister*'s link to a typical moviegoer; she portrays a nonchaser who finds herself caught in a tense tornado chase. As the scene plays over and over, De Bont murmurs his instructions to the ILM staffers: Darken this, lighten that . . . De Bont has watched mountains of videotapes and films of real-life tornadoes, and consulted with numerous scientists at the National Severe Storms Laboratory in Oklahoma; he has become a kind of tornado expert. If anyone in Hollywood knows what a movie twister should look like, it's De Bont.

Watching the video screen, you might think the tornado is the only digital effect in the scene. It isn't; there is another one, although you'd never guess it. Remember the damaged tractor with the spinning wheel? It *looks* like a real tractor, but it isn't. It's a complete digital illusion, manufactured in the computer and added to the scene after it was filmed. De Bont came up with the idea for the tractor after shooting a scene where a tractor was blown aloft. Wouldn't it be nice, he thought, to show what happened to the tractor? By then it was too late to go back to Oklahoma and reshoot the scene, but that's no problem in the digital age. In the comfort of an ILM office, digital artist John Stillman blended a computerized image of a tractor into a digitized reel of the movie footage. As an added touch, he made its wheel spin. The tractor effect passes so quickly that in the final film, most viewers may miss it entirely. Yet it's one of the countless subtle touches that give the film its gritty, realistic look.

Such "invisible" digital effects are increasingly common in films. You may have heard about the digitized feather that floats down from the sky and lands at the protagonist's feet in *Forrest Gump*. But there are many other examples, some so mundane that—like the tractor—you'd never suspect they were digitized. An advertising sign for Taco Bell, a company unfamiliar to non-U.S. audiences, was changed to a Pizza Hut sign for foreign releases of *Demolition Man*. Digital effects also allow a filmmaker to turn a few hundred cheering sports fans into a stadium packed with tens of thousands of people.

Naturally, some Hollywood veterans fear that digital technology will put a lot of crafts workers—lighting experts, model makers, and set designers, for example—out of work. Why build an elaborate stage set when you can digitize one in a computer? Why hire ten thousand extras when a few hundred can be cloned in the computer?

Twister's special physical effects boss, John Frazier, recalls that years ago, "I fought [digital effects] like everybody else and thought, 'Oh man, I've got to find another career.'" As it turned out, "what has happened is they're making *more* movies because of digital effects. *Twister* would never have been made without digital—it would still be on the shelf. So even though digital has taken some work from us, it has made *more* work than it has taken away."

De Bont says: "A lot of people are very worried about all these new technologies. But I think it's an *incredible* tool. The possibilities you have to 'paint' an image right now are *so* enhanced. In the past, the footage was totally dependent on what the [filming] situation was like. You didn't have *time* to wait until the weather was right, until it starts raining or hailing. *We* can create rain or hail whenever we want!"

Not without considerable effort, though. Digital work can be exhausting. "At times I go home and I want to cry, I'm so tired," Bromley said. "But the first time I saw a dinosaur on film, I knew filmmaking would never be the same."

To actors, digital filmmaking poses a special challenge. During the shooting of a film, they must react realistically to amazing sights—say, a tornado or a dinosaur—that aren't really there. Through the spring and summer of 1995, *Twister* leads Bill Paxton and Helen Hunt screamed and yelled and pointed at imaginary tornadoes in the empty Midwestern sky. The tornado images were added to the film months later by ILM's digital artists.

In one sense, Hunt and Paxton were doing what any actor does, whether it's in a blockbuster movie or a community dinner theater: simulating human emotions and behaviors in a simulated environment.

Paxton says: "I'm of the 'Jimmy Cagney' school—when I have to do an emotional scene, I just throw myself into it." Not without preparation, however: He psyched himself for *Twister*'s tensest scenes by watching a commercially available videotape, *Tornadoes: The Entity*. "It's an hour of tornado footage, and it's got this weird Philip Glass-type music throughout it. I just 'fed' all those images into my head." Paxton also participated in a tornado chase with a VORTEX team. For him, the road trip to the Texas panhandle was a trip down memory lane. He's a native of the Midwest and grew up in towns such as Fort Worth, Texas. "We passed by drive-in movies that I remembered taking teenage girls to. I'd say, 'Gosh, I remember taking Nan Brogan to that theater!'" He didn't see a tornado, though.

He also read numerous accounts of historic tornadoes, such as the ghastly Tri-State Tornado of 1925 that supposedly scattered human limbs around the countryside. "The Tri-State must have looked like four *Titanic*s coming at you," Paxton says. "The night before I met Jan [De Bont, the director], I just crammed my head with tornado stories. I was the first and only actor he saw for the part."

Twister is a harbinger of twenty-first-century filmmaking. What digital wonders will future moviegoers see? Will we see entirely digital worlds? Even digital actors? The Walt Disney film *Toy Story* is a sign that all-digital movies are not only technically feasible but can draw large audiences and critical acclaim.

History hints at what lies ahead. In 1968, Stanley Kubrick directed *2001: A Space Odyssey*, whose haunting special effects paved the way to the swarm of super-science-fiction films of the next two decades, notably George Lucas's *Star Wars* series. Likewise, the digital effects of mid-1990s films might lead, in the next century, to fantastic sights never before seen on the silver screen. One might say that *2001* inaugurated the age of realistic special effects, while 1993's *Jurassic Park* launched the age of *hyper*-realism. With the release of *Jurassic Park*, entire-screen digital images were at last indistinguishable from photographic reality. It's as if the dinosaurs were creatures in a National Geographic TV documentary. And ILM digital artists made *Jurassic Park*'s dinosaurs possible.

Where will it lead? Recently Lucas, ILM's owner, has championed the concept of the digital studio. Backdrops can be stored on computer disks, then digitally added to movie scenes whenever necessary. The result, Lucas says, could be a huge savings in money. Actors could, for instance, perform on a soundstage. Later a completely realistic-looking backdrop—say, a Hawaiian volcano or the white wasteland of Antarctica—could be digitally added to the scene. Filmmakers would be freer to pursue their cinematic visions, unconstrained by geography or finances.

Eventually, filmmakers may routinely use computers to bring actors such as Marilyn Monroe back to life on movie screens. Stars might even license their faces to filmmakers for use long after the actor is dead and buried. Where will it all end? Will Humphrey Bogart again walk the streets of San Francisco in *Maltese Falcon 2?*

"Instead of doing one movie a year, Arnold Schwarzenegger could do ten movies a year and still have time to have a wonderful life," Magid said. (Indeed, thanks to computers, a young girl's face was transposed onto the body of a stunt woman in a particularly harrowing scene in *Jurassic Park.*)

Thanks to computers, "conceivably, you could redo the ending of *Casablanca* so Bogie would leave Casablanca on the plane, or put John Wayne in Clark Gable's role in *Gone With the Wind,*" said film director Joe Dante (who made *Gremlins* and *Explorers*).

Ultimately, digital filmmaking enhances directors' ability to stir our deepest hopes and fancies. "The thing I like about visual effects is it's the art that most closely replicates your dream state," says Kim Bromley of ILM. "So you can have fairies flying around, or tornadoes in the distance, or cartoon characters come to life. . . . We can actually take these tools and make [a dream] real. And unlike a Salvador Dalí painting, you can attach sound to it and make it move."

A quarter of a century ago, the novelist John Fowles wrote:

"I saw my first film when I was six; I suppose I've seen on average—and discounting television—a film a week ever since; let's say some two and a half thousand films up to now. How can so frequently repeated an experience not have indelibly stamped itself on the *mode* of imagination? At one time I analyzed my dreams in detail; again and again I recalled purely cinematic effects . . . panning shots, close shots, tracking, jump cuts, and the like. In short, this mode of imagination is far too deep in me to eradicate—not only in me, in all my generation."

How will new film technologies affect future generations' "mode of imagination," as Fowles calls it? The power to depict any imaginable scene—no matter how eerie or unearthly—is a power that ancient peoples would have granted only to gods . . . or to demons. Now that power is in the hands of filmmakers. The tornadoes of *Twister* are, then, more than omens of future natural disasters. Those digitized funnels also point toward new, transcendent ways of seeing—even of *experiencing* life and nature—that storytellers and novelists and poets and musicians and painters have sought for millennia, usually in vain. Now, in the same century when humanity made outer space, Antarctica, and the ocean floor part of its backyard, it has also colonized those transcendent worlds—and all with the click of a mouse.

RECOMMENDED SOURCES

If you'd like to learn more about tornadoes and weather in general, here is a short list of useful sources. Please remember that addresses (both street addresses and World Wide Web URLs) are prone to change.

Magazines

Storm Track. Established in 1977, this lively magazine covers all the news that's news in the world of storm chasing. For subscription details, write editor Tim Marshall at 1336 Brazos Blvd., Lewisville, Texas 75067.

Weatherwise. A long-established bimonthly for weather buffs. It runs many articles on and advertisements for books and videotapes about severe weather. For subscription details, call 1-800-365-9753.

Videotapes

Numerous videotape collections of twister footage are for sale. They vary widely in quality and cost. This writer's favorite is *Tornado Video Classics I*, which includes thrilling footage of tornadoes and an excellent history of tornado research. For details, write The Tornado Project, Box 302, St. Johnsbury, VT 05819.

Books

Significant Tornadoes 1680–1991 (1993) by Thomas P. Grazulis. Advanced tornado buffs can profit from this very expensive but astonishing 1,326-page book by a tornado consultant to the Nuclear Regulatory Commission. The book describes every recorded tornado in U.S. history. It includes lengthy discussions of how tornadoes form and how scientists study them, plus numerous rare black-and-white photos. For details, write The Tornado Project, Box 302, St. Johnsbury, VT 05819.

Tornadoes (1989) by Ann Armbruster and Elizabeth A. Taylor, published by Franklin Watts. Written for middle school and high school students.

Tornadoes! (1994) by Lorraine Jean Hopping, published by Scholastic Inc. Written for grades two and three.

The Weather Book (1992) by Jack Williams. By far the best popular weather book available in the English language. Written by one of the founders of *USA Today*'s weather page, the book is rich in scientific detail and includes superb color illustrations.

Internet Sites

The Internet offers numerous weather discussion groups and World Wide Web sites.

If you have a computer and modem (ideally, at least 14,400 baud rate) you can explore the world of storm chasers at the Storm Chasers Homepage at

http://taiga.geog.niu.edu/chaser/chaser.html

The Homepage includes numerous photos of tornadoes.

The National Severe Storms Laboratory's Web site is

http://www.nssl.uoknor.edu